"I have laid aside business, and gone a-fishing."
—Izaak Walton, *The Compleat Angler*

The Sun Still Shines on a Dog's Ass

Stories

by Alan Good

Death of Print

Published by Death of Print in 2021
Deathofprint.press

Cover and book design by Alan Good
The main text typeface is Bembo Std.
Display text is Bodoni 72 Oldstyle.
Printed and distributed by IngramSpark.

Print ISBN: 978-0-9981710-2-9
Ebook ISBN: 978-1-0879-7097-4

"Sahara's Law" first appeared in *The Blotter*. "Fireworks at Midnight," "Pallet King," and "That Time I Was a Cop" appeared in *The Gallimaufry*. "Taxidermy the Rich" appeared in *Back Patio*. "Walnuts" appeared in *Neutral Spaces*. "The Sun Still Shines on a Dog's Ass" was serialized in the author's newsletter, *Unagented Trash*. "Practice Shot" and "Timewarp" are previously unpublished.

Sahara's Law

Part 1: I'm Oqueso – You're Oqueso

I saw a billboard with the word queso on it and decided to move to Texas. Texas is a fucked up, reactionary helltopia but you can put queso on whatever you want down here.

I didn't know a single person in Texas, which made it all the more appealing. There's only two reasons anyone would choose to live in Texas: because you're running away from someone—and queso. I read on the internet, meaning I made this up, that men think about sex more than six thousand times per day. I am a man for queso. I knew I would be safe in Texas because no one who was mad at me would be mad enough or care enough to look for me in Texas.

I figured I would feel at home in Amarillo because I've also mispronounced my own name. It was when I met Brad, dreamy, jut-jawed, abtastic Brad, the first time and he said, "Hey. I'm Brad." And I did a pathetic little wave and said, "Sarah," but because I was choking on my own nervousness it sounded more like "Sahara." For eight months, all through our courtship and engagement, up until that last day when I snapped and said, "Actually, Brad, it's 'Sarah.' Not 'Sahara,' just 'Sarah.' Sair. Uh.," he called me Sahara. I even changed my voicemail to "Hey this is Sahara leave a message at the bleeeeeeeeeeeeeeeep." I thought it was funny to say "bleeeeeeeeeeeeeeeep" like my voicemail was me swearing on the radio, but he was always saying I needed to change it so I'd sound more professional. Maybe, I always wanted to say, I could just say my real name. That would sound more professional.

I got a second-floor apartment with a balcony that looked over the Arbor Trail into the parking lot of a Red Roof Inn and beyond that was the big road, I-40, which runs all the way from wherever it starts out to Barstow, California. The apartment wasn't great, but it had pool access and was a tenth of New York rent and I didn't have to share it with the guy from *American Psycho*. Amarillo's water tastes like if you find a half-empty bottle of water in your backpack and when you take a sip you remember that you bought it like nine months ago, drank half of it, dunked a half-smoked cigarette in it because Brad was about to catch you smoking, put the lid back on, shoved it in the darkest depths of your backpack, and forgot about it. I discovered by accident that it didn't taste quite as foul if

I brushed my teeth before taking a drink and now my teeth are shiny.

I didn't socialize much, but that didn't stop all the white women in Texas from asking me why I wasn't married and pregnant. I would have run away again, but I didn't want to break my lease. I wondered for a minute why only white women wanted me to get pregnant, and then I asked myself this question: if you weren't white, would you give a shit if white people were having babies? The answer was I wouldn't want very many of them to have babies. I don't want babies and I don't understand why anyone wants to have babies or why anyone wants other people, especially white people, to have babies. They're cute, sure, but have you seen what happens to them? There's too many humans on this planet anyway, and a third of all American babies born today are going to grow up thinking that whoever the future version of Tim Allen is is funny.

I got a job working in the shoe department of the local outlet of a regional sporting goods retailer called The Jock's Trap. I was completely unqualified because I hate shoes, feet, and humans, but the manager hired me anyway because her daughter had just gone off to college and she wanted a lost victim to mother. She was always looking after me, checking in on me, calling me hon, saying what I really needed was a good man and unfortunately there just weren't none to be had.

People would ask me about shoes, questions like what's the difference between whatever shoes they were holding up as if trying to balance the scales of justice, and I would say, "I unno" or "Them ones're cheaper" in my offensive approximation of Texas dialect. Occasionally I'd give a bullshit answer like "These Adoodas got the patented turbo leather injected maxipad foam jumpstart soles," which usually impressed the customers. I was always supposed to promote the add-ons. Cleaning foam. Some wand thing that's supposed to erase dirt and scuffmarks from the sides of the soles. This stupid protective waterproofing spray. They called these after-sales and I sucked at them and every day Claire, my boss, would remind me to push the add-ons, you've got to push the add-ons, but I never did, and I never got fired or disciplined, which I wouldn't have minded because it would have at least mixed up my routine. After every shift I went to this fast-food Tex–Mex joint in the food court called the Americantina and ate queso like it was soup.

I was wrong. Someone was looking for me. I opened the balcony door and when I stepped outside a snake landed on my head. Welcome to Texas, home of table-sized steaks, putting creationist museums next to important paleontological sites, and snakes that fly but aren't very good at it. I'm sure there's a rational explanation for how a snake fell on my face but my version fits my motif. The lucky thing for me insofar as one is able to use the word "lucky" in relation to being snaked on from above is that it wasn't a Western diamondback rattlesnake and if it had been it probably would have still been too discombobulated to bite me. Maybe not, since when I googled "rattlesnakes of texas" to find out what kinds of rattlesnakes live in Texas I found a story about the decapitated head of a Western diamondback rattlesnake that bit a man and nearly killed him, so clearly for rattlesnakes there's no such thing as being too discombobulated to bite a stupid human. (I typed "rattlesnack" instead of "rattlesnake" just now, which is definitely a sign from the universe.) A man said my name. As if flailing on my balcony while trying to fling off a snake that had already bounced off my face, landed on my ratty lawn chair, and hurled itself to freedom in the landscaping rocks below wasn't discombobulating enough, a strange man was calling my name.

"Ms. Tassell?" he said.

I stopped flailing and looked at him, blankly, trying to decide whether I should run inside and barricade the door or fling myself to my death.

"Are you Ms. Sarah Tassell?"

He checked the paper on his clipboard. He looked like a used-car salesman, dressed in an ill-fitting suit with a giant red tie, all Texaned up in cowboy boots and a black Stetson. I don't really know if it was a Stetson; Stetson is just the only brand of cowboy hat I know. I believe the term for that is metonymy or something but I got a C in lit crit so I wouldn't listen to me. Statistics were on the side of him being a used-car salesman, since aside from working in oil and/or gas all the jobs in Amarillo are mainly retail, food service, or being a used-car salesman, but there was something about him that suggested he wasn't really a used-car salesman. Whatever he did for a living, whoever had sent him there looking for me, I didn't want to talk to him.

"I just want to ask you a few questions," he said. "I won't take up much of your time," he said.

When he went around the corner to walk up the stairs that led to my door I climbed over the railing and, mad snake in the rocks be damned, jumped into the juniper bush outside my downstairs neighbors' balcony. I didn't die or even break anything. I ran as fast and as far as I could, which was to a restaurant that used to be a gas station up on Wolflin, the nearest road to my apartment. To be fair, it's a wonky road and it jogs away from my building so it wasn't like I just ran for a hundred feet and stopped. More like a hundred yards.

And that's when I discovered gravy. At a dirty-looking restaurant called Restaurant in West Amarillo. I said to the nine-hundred-year-old waitress, "What is chicken-fried steak? Is it chicken or steak?" She grabbed a plate of it off the neighboring table and showed me what it looks like.

"It's cow meat," she said. "Chicken-fried."

"OK," I said. "Can I get that with queso?"

"Don't got no queso," she said, very unTexanlike, "but it come with gravy."

"Oh," I said. "Does gravy have cheese in it?"

"You a vegetarian?" she said.

"I just ordered the chicken-fried cow meat."

"Just checking. You coulda been a vegan. Vegans don't consume anything that come from a animal."

Not much time passed before she plopped a plate on the table before me. There on the plate were some disintegrating green beans, a turdpile-covered-in-snow-esque mound of mashed potatoes, and the aforementioned chicken-fried cow meat. She set down a bowl of gravy.

"I put your gravy on the side, case you was a vegan."

"So it does have cheese," I said excitedly.

"Nah."

Humans are overrated, but gravy is not. Gravy is a gift from the gods. How had I lived my whole life without gravy? For the first time in my life I felt resentment toward my parents. They loved me, they cared for me, they read to me, sent me to good schools and didn't burden me with a sibling, but I'll never forgive them for depriving me of gravy.

I have a love-hate relationship with food: I love food and I hate myself and everyone else and pretty much everything except food.

I was vegetarian for about nine years, until I realized no one else really cares about animals or the planet or their bodies or anything, no one else is trying to be a good person, so why should I deny myself bacon? At any minute I might get shot dead in the street or the mall or at work or a party or a picnic or a school or a movie theater or a gas station or a bank or a fair or a restaurant or a concert or a sidewalk or a church or a parking lot or a public restroom or my home. At any minute I might get run down by a van or blown up at a community event or crushed by an out-of-control satellite, or something more mundane might happen like I could get strangled or beaten or trampled or stabbed or macheteed or raped and murdered, raped and murdered and raped again, or raped and decapitated like a discombobulated snake. I take the long view: I'll be a vegetarian for trillions of years when I'm dead.

Even today, even with my new yen for gravy and queso, I could definitely be a vegan if cheese had never been invented. But cheese has been invented and if the government ever banned cheese, and there's really no telling what the government's going to do anymore, I would become a cheese outlaw, engaging in gruyèrilla warfare, milking cows and goats in underground dairies, learning secret knocks and handshakes as I bootleg brie to the oppressed cheese lovers of America. Brad and I were just back from a five-mile run when I decided to leave him. He wanted to make us a smoothie using something called kefir.

"What's kefir?"

"It's the champagne of yogurt. It's drinkable yogurt. It's super good for you. Loads of probiotics."

I almost started crying. Instead I just said, "It's bullshit that kefir is good for you and ice cream isn't."

He had us on this keto diet so we would look good for our wedding photos and his sperm would be super healthy and strong. You're not allowed to eat bread because the keto diet was created by the devil. Keto. Kefir. Motherfucking quinoa. He said he wanted to live forever. Have you not heard anyone talking about what this stupid world is going to look like in eighty years? You live forever and put up with the mega hurricanes and the desertification and the killer drones, and I'll eat bread and die young. We'll both be happy.

I'm not happy. Happiness is bullshit. Every day is a nightmare. I want to live forever.

I thought the strange man was an emissary of Brad's, but when I got home I saw, from the flyer he left on my door, that he just wanted to invite me to join his cult. I was relieved but also hurt. I can never want to see Brad again, want him to never try to look for or contact me, but also be upset that he's not trying to look for or contact me. It's not a contradiction; it's just human. Fuck that bastard.

The second-most-common question the white women of Texas asked me was what church I went to and then how come I didn't go to church. Usually I gave a noncommittal answer like I just don't hrmpfh fjlk;lkj fsjlk;a eeee, but once I revealed myself as a formidable theologian. "I don't mean to upend your whole worldview or anything," I said to Anna Lee Lee, who lived in my apartment complex and always seemed to check the mail at the same time as me even though I always looked to make sure she wasn't anywhere in sight before I ventured out to the mailbox, "but if God is all-powerful and all-loving, why aren't nachos a superfood?" She's an atheist now.

If you don't wear sunscreen the sun will turn you into ash like a vampire, but if you buy the wrong sunscreen your skin will poison you or a coral reef, probably both. If you drive a car you're polluting the air and accelerating global warming, and if you fly on a plane you might as well buy five F150s and let their engines idle during an ozone alert until they run out of gas. The air outside will make you sick. The air inside will make you sick because we like the organic compounds used in our paints and household cleaners like we like the personalities of our former child stars: volatile. Everything is destroying the planet and everything gives you cancer. The last time I went to California I almost turned around because the welcome sign said "WARNING: The state of California contains chemicals known to the state of California to cause cancer." Sometimes I feel like saying fuck it I'm just going to live inside one of those bubbles but I know the bubble would be made out of BPA plastic. I went to Texas because I wanted to not care anymore and it just seemed like a place where you could ignore all the ethical dilemmas that make modern life an unnavigable labyrinth of monstrousness and still feel like you're a good person. I know that sounds like a dig at Texas, but I also mean that any place is like that, just a little more in Texas, because everything's a little more in Texas.

I always thought of Texas as a wasteland and it is but it's also incredibly beautiful if you can see past the oil rigs and used-car lots and the billboards for oil rigs and used-car lots. Just thinking of the time I saw a longhorn standing in a sea of bluebonnets makes me cry.

One thing I liked to do with Brad was replace the word far with fart, as in "No, Brad, not tonight because I had to walk really fart today and I'm tired." Or "Hey I wonder how fart it is from Earth to Uranus." He never reacted. I could never tell if he wasn't paying attention or he was too confused or offended to say anything. I'm saying fart every time I mean far and it doesn't bother you? It doesn't annoy you or make you laugh or want to grab me and shake me and say why the fart I mean why the fuck do you keep saying fart instead of far? Have a fucking reaction, Brad.

Part 2: The Queso the Expostulating Flashturbator

We're past the point of the story where something is supposed to happen. Something did happen. I was organizing the shoe wall one night before close and Claire came over to me and said, "Hon, I just wanted to warn you to be on the lookout for perverts cuz I heard there was a flashturbator on the loose." I didn't say what in the name of Christmas is a flashturbator because even though I'd never heard the word before I knew exactly what it meant. So what? Dudes jerk off in public all the time. I've seen more men jerking off in public in my life than I've read Margaret Atwood novels and I double-majored in Women's Studies and English at Hunter College. One time I leant forward to drink from a public water fountain and saw a pool of fresh cum blobbing around the drain. A giggling teenage boy giggled maniacally and ran from his hiding spot behind the section of books about Nazis at the main branch of the New York Public Library. I've never understood the women who complained about guys not giving up their seats or men spreading out on the subway to take up more than one seat. Why would you even think about sitting down on the subway? Do you have any idea how much semen is coating the subway seats? That's not laquer, it's gallons and gallons of jizz that's hardened in the summer heat and fused with the plastic of the seats. Even Brad, my very respectable fiancée, ex-fiancée, Brad the born-again-again successful lawyer slash future senator, was on a mission to masturbate in public in all fifty U.S. states and on all seven continents and even, fingers crossed, on Mars if he can get in good with Elon Musk. That's my big fear, that he'll find me by accident, that I'll turn the corner and there he'll be pumping his pecker next to the giant rolling cow outside The Big Texan, scratching another state off his cumbucket list. Claire was the first boss I had who didn't try to masturbate in front of me, although one time I walked in to the break room and she was vigorously scratching her butthole. Even then I was able to back away and I don't think she knew I saw her. Men jerking off in public was as common in New York as almost stepping on dog poop and I didn't expect Amarillo to be any different. But it was. It was organized.

People think I'm crazy. Brad was a catch, is what everyone told me. They didn't know him like I did. He didn't abuse me, physically or emotionally, aside from the fact that thinking about having his children made me want to kill myself and yet he continued to tell me how much he wanted to put a baby in me. He would say it like that, "God, Sahara, I want to put a baby in you. Oh Sahara, Sahara," while trying to kiss me, and I'd say something like, "Hey, did you know you can get on the train and be in Delaware in like an hour? I'm pretty sure you've never masturbated in Delaware. Oh man my boss just texted and so-and-so called in sick gotta go sorry."

As you might have guessed, I encountered a flashturbator. It's all probability. If a flashturbator is active in your area and you have tits and/or a vagina and are under fifty, the odds of encountering said flashturbator are very much in your favor. Especially if your town is plagued with an epidemic of flashturbators, as mine was.

I had just finished my shift and was heading for my queso fix when this guy jumped out from behind one of those food court trash cans and started jerking off at me. Not in front of me, at me. "Your hair is so," he said, and paused, "red."

I did something then out of context. I confronted him. I don't like confrontation, but I also don't like walking around wondering if someone is about to shove a dick in my face.

I wanted to cringe and run to the security kiosk. Instead I said, "Excuse me, but what the fuck are you doing?"

Masturbating creepy dude gets confronted in food court. What happens next will shock you!

He goes, "I am praising my personal Lord and Savior, Jesus Christ."

"Uh," I said, and I'm fully aware you're not supposed to include uhs in dialogue, but that's what I said, "what the fuck does that mean?"

"What the fuck?" could replace the five Ws. Ninety percent of crime could be solved by just flat-out asking people what the fuck are you doing.

I asked. He answered. "Name's Jake," he said. "I belong to an ancient sect of Christianity called the Gnosdicks and we celebrate our faith through communing with our members."

"Your members? You mean you jerk off for Jesus."

"That's a rather," pausing as his eyes rolled in the back of his head and he pulled a face like someone had just shoved a whole peeled lemon covered with cayenne pepper in his mouth, "crude way to put it."

"How many people are in your sect?"

"We are a small group of true believers. Small but growing. Small but powerful."

"So it's just you?"

"Twenty-six. There's twenty-six of us, okay. I'm worshipping right now, so if you could stay where you are because I have a thing for flat-chested redheads but also be quiet that would be oooooom great thanks."

"That's bullshit. This isn't a thing. You dummies made this up to give yourselves an excuse to jerk off in public."

"That's not true," he said, looking like it definitely was true. "Anyway, if women can breastfeed in public men should be allowed to tug our dicks in public, too. That's what equal rights means!"

"That's not true at all."

"Listen," he said, "God made man in His image, in *His* image, and he made woman from man. That means woman is subservient to man. If God made men in His image that means God has a dick. So we celebrate that aspect of God that has been ignored due to PC censorship. We honor the Lord by celebrating the thing that men alone share with him, the sacred phallus."

Then he closed his eyes, lifted his face toward the sky, that is, the food court ceiling, and quoted the Bible at me while still jerking off at me. "This is from 2 Samuel," he said, "book six, verses twenty to twenty-two:

> As soon as David returned home to bless his own household, Saul's daughter Michal came out to meet him. "How the king of Israel has distinguished himself today!" she said. "He has uncovered himself today in the sight of the maidservants of his subjects, like a vulgar person would do." But David said to Michal, "I was dancing before the LORD who chose me over your father and all his house when He appointed me ruler over the LORD's people Israel. I will celebrate before the LORD, and I will humiliate and humble myself even more than this. Yet I will be honored by the maidservants of whom you have spoken."

"Like King David, I will celebrate before the Lord," Jake said. "By the way, do you know what happens to Michal? That bitch is barren. For her impiousness she is cursed with childlessness. 'And Michal the daughter of Saul had no children to the day of her death.' So watch out, cunt."

I had one of those stupid cleaning wands in my pocket and I pulled it out halfway hoping he would think it was pepper spray and said, "What a bunch of shit. Isn't the Bible against masturbation? Spilling your seed and unclean discharge and stuff like that?"

"That line has historically been willfully and maliciously misinterpreted by heretics and radical feminists, of which I can see you is both."

"Whatever," I said, and I took a picture of him with my phone and jogged off to the security kiosk, where I was told to call the police if I wanted to report a crime but mall security was not about to interfere with the free expression of an individual's religion.

When a cop finally showed up the jerkoff in the food court was gone. I told the cop what happened and explained about the Gnosdicks and he said, "Oh them, they harmless. They just expressing they religious freedom."

I jammed my phone with the evidentiary dick pic up in his face and that's when I noticed that Jake and the cop were both wearing the same lapel pin, which had a design on it that looked like this:

Part 3: Sahara's Law: A Queso Study

Like an evil entity from a Japanese horror movie that gets remade, but really badly, for an English-speaking audience, the Gnosdicks started out on the internet and moved into the real world when they felt brave and powerful enough, thanks to the rise of neofascism, to pull their dicks out in the mall. The image on the cop's lapel pin was the official Gnosdick symbol, according to the official Gnosdick website, which is the only place on the entire internet with any mention of the Gnosdicks, which I guess makes me optimistic. Their website was pretty thin, a few rants written by an anonymous poster who was probably Jake, but mostly just links to Jordan Peterson videos, which made me feel better about my decision to leave Brad without a word or a note or a forwarding address. When he came home with *12 Rules for Life* I knew I only had six weeks, which is how long it takes him to read a book, before he tried to kill me. I also read on the internet, I'm not making this up, either, about a boy in Texas who found a rattlesnake wriggling out of a toilet in his house, and then two more rattlesnakes wriggled out behind the first one, and it turned out there were more than twenty rattlesnakes under the house. I already had a phobia about sitting on the toilet before I read that story. Just think, the same God who made us and claims to love us also made rattlesnakes and showed them the secret entrance to our houses.

From my experience, everyone in Texas is crazy. Like that *Midnight in the Garden of Good and Evil* kind of crazy. My neighbor lady, for instance, thought she was on a diet if she only ate breakfast at The Donut Stop every *other* morning. And even as he was speaking words that would have only made sense if they were part of a parody of men's rights activists, that Gnosdickhead Jake I think really believed his own malarkey. And I thought if you ate right and exercised and voted for the right people everything would be okay somehow. I guess that's not so much crazy as stupid. Before you judge, you have to consider the psychological pressures acting on every Texan. You might be sitting in one of those beautiful lethargic brown rivers one minute, afraid to get your nose in the water because that's how the brain-infecting amoebas get to your brain in order to infect it, on a summer day featuring Venuslike temperatures, just enjoying the shit out of your life, and the next minute a swirling death cloud can descend from the sky and suck you right out of your swimsuit. You don't exist in tornado country without doing real damage to your psyche. I want to buy one of those annoying loud pickup trucks and a trailer just so I can haul around a tornado shelter everywhere I go.

Being a woman anywhere is a lot like living in tornado country. This law doesn't apply quite as broadly to men, but for women, especially those of us who live in America and other "underdeveloped" countries, it's almost universal: spend enough time on this planet and you will be raped, murdered, and/or abducted. Quite possibly all three. It happened to me, the abduction part, though for a while there I did expect to hit the trifecta. One minute I was following Claire out to the loading dock because she wanted to show me a bird's nest she found because she knew I liked animals, only it was a mythical bird's nest that turned out to be just a device to get me out to the loading dock so some Bible-quoting cocktivist could throw a burlap sack over my head and shove me into a metal dog kennel that was welded onto a flatbed truck, and the next minute I was all sack-headed and pretzeled up in the back of a hot metal dog kennel. To me, that kind of truck is a major red flag and anyone driving one should be pulled over and searched, the decision to purchase a rolling abduction machine being probable cause enough, but I'm told they're popular among sportsmen, who take their bird dogs out to the wilderness or canned hunt ranches to hunt birds and shit.

As it turned out, Jake and his weird band of phallophiles were just men's rights extremists and duplicitous Claire was in on it. They had this grand scheme to kidnap wayward women and deprogram us from the feminist propaganda they say dominates American culture and reprogram us to respect men again, and by respect they mean worship and make ourselves subservient to men. Claire was a "getter." She hired vulnerable women to be deprogrammed, reprogrammed, and repopulated, a process they termed ReWomaning.

"How could you do this?" I said to traitorous Claire when I saw her in the basement of Jake's mom's house where I and three other young women, a brunette and two blondes, were being held. All of us were white because in addition to being stupid and misogynistic our captors were also white supremacists, only interested in "saving" white women, with whom they thought they were going to rebuild and repopulate Western (aka white) civilization.

"I thought we were friends," I said to Claire, even though I never thought that. "I thought you liked me."

"Not really. You're rude and selfish and all you talk about is queso and you're a terrible worker. Easily the worst employee I ever had. I knowed you'd be a terrible worker when I hired you but I also knowed you was an obvious candidate for ReWomaning. I don't like you the way you are now, a childless, godless, manophobic hussy," she said with a frown, "but I'm sure we'll be friends soon," she said with a smile.

"Can I still use you as a reference?"

"God no."

"You evil fucking bitch."

"Oh my, that's a good sign. Already using misogynistic epithets. That's a hopeful sign, hon. I think if we can scrub the f-word out your filthy mouth, hon, we can have you debugged and rebooted and back on the street faster 'n you can say 'God bless the patriarchy.'"

Which gave me an idea.

There was no point in screaming, the other ladies told me. The basement was soundproofed for Jake's podcast about religious-themed video games, his favorite being this one called *Glory's Sword* where you are the angel of death cutting down the sinners at the apocalypse. That's all there is, no strategy, no challenge, no levels, you're just walking around with fancy wings and a bigass sword chopping off the heads of heretics and radical feminists. Jake was really good at it.

They read us a lot of Bible verses about how penises are good and women are the property of their husbands and if a man rapes a virgin woman he just has to pay off the girl's dad and he's all set. We were blasted with country music, told to love Jesus and Kenny Chesney. Taught to be grateful for compliments about our tits and asses. Encouraged to pursue careers in nursing, elementary education, and "homekeeping." They read to us descriptions of women by dickblessed (Gnosdickian for male) writers of thrillers and mysteries, mainly James Patterson. Women who were cool and sensuous and eminently fuckable in the direst of straits. The heroine is dangling from a water tower, underneath her is a pit of vipers and alligators, but her flowing red hair still radiates like a supernova, leaving the reader to wonder not whether or how she will escape her deadly predicament but whether her pubes are red, too. In case you're wondering about my pubes, by the way, fuck off. We had to become such women, held captive by fanatic men who viewed all sex initiated by themselves as consensual, yet maintaining our poise, or in my case faking a poise I had never poisessed. All I wanted to do was poop my pants but I had to play sexy.

We had to smile, act coy, and bat our eyes or our eyelashes or whichever it is, at wolf whistles and catcalls. I remember this guy came into the store, he was walking by but he stopped and walked backward and came in the store just to say to me, "Ooh, honey, your hair's so red it could run for governor as a Republican and have my vote. *Lord.*" And I guess, according to the teachings of Gnosdickism, instead of pretending like I didn't hear him I should have said, "Thank you, sir, would you like to yank it or rub your nose all in it?"

My idea was I just went along with everything. I submitted, or pretended to submit, to all their stupid brainwashing. This section would have been a lot longer, but I can't describe in detail the full horror of our experience because the ReWomaning Process is trademarked and I really don't want to get sued. I'm already worried I've described too much. The first thing I had to do after the burlap sack came off my head was sign a non-disclosure agreement. The point is it was creepy and scary and we were terrified but we

29

acted nice and ignorant and interested and laughed at their shitty jokes in the hope that they wouldn't cut our tits and heads off.

Through it all I submitted. I asked no questions. Did everything they asked. They were so proud of me. When, after five terrifying days of submission and smiling and oh God you're right, Jakes, I was deemed "fit for decent society," they let me go, set me up with a job as a secretary at a used-car place.

I went straight to the police, of course, making sure to avoid the cop from the mall. They finally let me talk to a detective, who said, "Oh, we know them people. They harmless. You sure you want to press charges? It's a lotta hassle."

"Yes, goddamnit."

"Hey now, let's keep it civil, hon."

If I sound sort of blasé about all this, it's just my way, but I was pretty pissed off and fucked up over it. Even though the Gnosdicks were all idiots and completely incompetent and their reprogramming program was halfassed horseshit it was a horrific experience and we all thought we were going to be murdered. For the record, all of us survived without being raped or murdered, although we still live in one of the rapiest, murderiest countries on Earth so we'll never really be safe. I probably still am fucked up over it. For instance, I'm opposed to the death penalty, but I was also disappointed, on the verge of outrage, when Claire and Jake and a couple of their cohorts were sentenced not to hanging or castration but to just a few months in minimum security. Castration would have been good for the guys not just because of the irony of their dick worship causing their dicks to get chopped off but also because the Bible says, in Neuteronomy 23:1, "If a man's testicles are crushed or his penis is cut off, he may not be admitted to the assembly of the LORD," which is pretty harsh of the Bible. Just when a man needs the LORD the most he is cut off not only from his junk but from his church.

You could say something good came out of this experience, aside from me shutting down a disgusting kidnapping ring and getting no credit for it, because after Claire went to prison I got rehired at The Jock's Trap and promoted to her position as manager, except I didn't want the responsibility so I quit.

Sometimes I stare out at the Red Roof Inn listening to the drone of the interstate and I think about taking it all the way to California, only I'd need a car for that and I don't want the responsibility and I sure as hell ain't going to hitchhike. Not gonna push my luck any farter. I could take the bus, of course, but Texas really isn't that bad. Texans seem ridiculously proud of their state, like in an almost phony way, but I guess it's normal for people to be over-proud of things they like that other people think are put here by Satan to remind us that Earth could have been awesome if the people who lived on it had been nicer. Whatever you might think of Texas, it is the American capital of queso and gravy, and that's something to be proud of. And where else am I going to get an apartment with pool access for this price? Nowhere, that's where.

Taxidermy the Rich

This rich fucker hit on top of us. I'll give him some credit because we was a good two hundred thirty yards from the tee and he hit a ball down the middle of the fairway that bounced about twenty feet short of where we was standing and would have rolled another thirty, forty yards if I hadn't knocked it down. Jess said we should let him play through, it wasn't worth starting anything. "Play through my ass," I said, and she goes, "That don't even make sense. Just let him play through."

All I'd wanted was a quick nine but this guy had to turn up. Fucker had on these white shorts that seemed to be swallowing a salmon polo shirt. Looked like an albino python trying to choke down a yuppie. After the country club got ripped up by that F-4 the collared-shirt crowd took over the pleb course with the express intent of reminding us that golf is their game. These country club boys didn't like the way we played. Didn't like the way we looked, our trucker hats and cutoff shirts. They wanted to install a dress code. Always in a goddamn hurry. What's the point of living in Oklahoma if you can't take a minute to finish your beer before lining up your putt? They was always on our asses, making snotty comments when they played through. They all had brand-name clubs and woods with heads as big as their egos.

I'd been fixing to let his ass play through but his breach of etiquette shot my good intentions straight to shit. Another day, I might've just stared him down and played on after I made my point, but I was wound tight. I'd only come out to get my muscles moving, get some of that negative energy out, clear my head of all the stress that was being heaped on me by rich fuckers just like him. Jess wanted to let it go, but it was her he was hitting on top of; some guys still didn't like to see women on the course, thought they couldn't play, and in spite of all their superficial gentlemanly ways they'd ride their ass and make demeaning jokes and treat them like second-class citizens, even Jess, who could drive a ball farther than me.

He weren't him but he looked just like that developer, the motherfucker that wanted to turn my farm into a gated community. Private security. Manicured yards. Cloned homes. A heated private "community" pool. A clubhouse. All these fucking libertarians think taxation is slavery and true liberty is only found in HOA fees. I wanted to hurt him. I wanted to sprint the two-and-a-thirds football fields that lay between us. I would hold my club up like a warrior leading his army into battle and bring it down on his skull and twist the staff around his neck. But I had no army. No one could make a fucking living farming anymore and I was the last holdout. I wanted to rip his heart out through his mouth. I wanted to drag him over to Formaldehyde Frank's place. Frank did taxidermy in his garage and I'd let him stuff the rich fucker and then I'd take him home and mount him at the end of the driveway, a scarecrow for when the developer comes back around.

I started toward him, raised my club and half-lunged, but I stopped myself. If I killed that rich fucker then the other rich fuckers would win. I'd get the death penalty and they'd get my farm.

I tossed my pitching wedge in the grass and pulled out my 5-wood.

Jess goes "Hey, what the fuck?"

I picked up the rich fucker's ball. A Top Flight that no one had ever had to dig out of a water hazard. I whacked it back at him. I'm pretty wild off the tee but I'm normally pretty straight with the 5-wood. This one I hooked further to the left than Che Guevara. I put a little too much into it. I don't know if he was scared, or if he just had enough sense not to push me, but he just flipped me off and trotted into the next fairway to hunt his ball and Jess and I played on. Jess beat my ass. Fucker had me rattled and I finished seven-over.

Pallet King

Ben was always saying you gotta start stockpiling pallets now. The building material of the future. Learn a little masonry and you can build out of stone but you won't be able to get Portland cement when the world ends. I tried to tell him you could use cob for the mortar, and you could build a whole house out of cob if you wanted, which I'd read about in *Mother Earth News* back when I was trying to make a go of farming, but he didn't hear me. He never seemed to hear me.

Pallets were ideal because you'd always be able to scrounge them. You could build with them intact or you could bust them apart. I spent many a Sunday at his place, using his old spud bar to pry the boards off, then hammering the nails out. He saved the gnarled old nails in Folgers cans in case he was ever called upon to build a pressure cooker bomb. The nails were for shrapnel. As far as I know he was never called upon but he sure did have the supply.

I got the call on a Sunday. I felt bad because I hadn't gone over that day. I felt bad because I hadn't gone over on a lot of Sundays. I'm still glad I didn't have to be the one to find him. It was his neighbor Ann that did. "It's your dad," she said. "He died. He's dead. He shot himself, Paul. You shoulda seen the—lord, sorry. I just thought you should know. The police are here. The coroner is on his way. I don't know, hon. I don't know."

"We gotta have a system," he had told me. "We gotta designate a meeting place. It's just a matter of time before this society crumbles but you and me are gonna be okay. We're gonna rebuild civilization."

"You and me?" I wanted to tell him he was the least civilized person I knew but I never had the nerve to tell him any of the things I really wanted to say. I had been unfair to him in my youth, I had told him too many of the things I really wanted to say, and I always felt bad about it. I was always trying to make it up to him but I never tried hard enough.

"Obviously the first option should be my place. It's the safest, the most secure, the most well stocked. But as a backup, if my place is under siege or otherwise unavailable, I say we meet out by the falls."

"The falls? You mean to tell me you think if things are so bad your little fortified compound isn't safe enough to inhabit that we'll be able to make it all the way out to the falls?"

"You got a better suggestion?"

"The falls." It didn't matter that if civil war broke out he'd last about an hour or that I couldn't be counted on to risk my life to save his or that I had half a mind to sell out and move to California. Nothing mattered. Nothing I said would matter so I just said "The falls."

We didn't have a funeral. I didn't want to organize one. It was enough work just picking out a casket and a plot and trying to make sense of all his papers. I was outside of myself. I was the one that died and I was watching it all from outside my body. I didn't know who to call. The family was all spread out and his friends were all nutcases. I wasn't sure which of them had already died of heart failure and which ones were still creeping along. If he had died a couple years later we could have blamed the lack of a funeral on the covid, although all the guys who were mad about me not giving the old man a funeral probably ended up being no-mask-wearing pandemic-deniers. They probably would have been even madder at me. There's no way to win. That's the main thing life has taught me.

Anyway the boys were pissed. They showed up one day when I was doing inventory, which consisted mostly of counting Ben's guns. I knew he'd been collecting them but I had no idea the extent. I didn't know where the hell he'd gotten the money for all these guns. He was just a recently retired gym teacher. Pistols. Shotguns. Rifles, the big ones that people have Opinions about. Magazines. Cases and cases of ammo. I couldn't have imagined how much it was all worth. Guns retain their value like pretty much nothing else. "Always keep the box," he had told me once. He was showing off this pretty new .22 he'd bought and I was pretending to give a shit. "These collectors love to see the box. And the original paperwork. They'll pay more for a gun with a box." All those years I had collected baseball cards, laboring under the delusion they'd be worth something one day, giddily picturing myself cashing in my Ken Griffey rookie for a flashy car one day, I should have been collecting guns. The boys had come en masse with an eye toward beating the shit out of me or just putting a little scare into me, depending on which one of them you asked, but Ben's arsenal mollified them.

There was Monkey and there was Dub and there was Ron and Jon and Don. They were dressed like an LL Bean swat team. Monkey was the mean one. The instigator. The others they just wanted companionship. A club to belong to. But Monkey wanted war. There was death in his eyes. He owned a zero turn lawnmower dealership. I don't know what the others all did but they all had the kinds of jobs where they could pretend to be working class while still making enough money to buy RVs and custom ARs.

Monkey told me I was a traitor for not giving the old man a proper funeral and if it was up to him they'd string me up by one of Ben's heavy duty extension cords, walk me up a gallows made of pallets, and let me swing. I didn't have any kind of response to that, not even to point out that I was big enough and young enough still to whoop all their asses combined. He emphasized his point by picking an axe off the table and throwing it twenty feet or so across the room. It stuck in this target Ben had made out of a pallet. Missed the bullseye by about a foot. Hatchet-throwing had got real popular for some reason lately.

Don, I think it was, although it could have been Jon, said "Don't pay him too much attention, Paul. Monkey likes to talk tough but deep down he's just an old softie."

"He's got a secret weakness," said Dub, and all of them except Monkey started chuckling.

Monkey said "Shut your mouth, Dub."

Dub laughed him down and said, "The national anthem. Dude can't listen to more than four bars before he breaks down crying."

"Shut up."

"It's true," said Dub. "Ain't nothing to be ashamed of. You're a patriot is all."

Ben had a three-bedroom house on his one-acre lot but he spent most of his time in the shop. It was a 1,500-square-foot metal building with twelve-foot ceilings. All the furniture in the shop was pallets. Workbenches. Chairs. He'd insulated the walls and closed them in with pallet boards and license plates.

Outside there was a pallet picnic table and several pallet deck chairs and a pallet chaise longue.

"We'll be safe here," he once told me. "This is my fortress." All around the property ran an eight-foot-high wall made of pallets. I'd helped him build that wall. I set every post. By then he'd had a couple heart attacks and didn't have the strength to dig a post hole. We slid each pallet over a four-by-four treated post and screwed the pallets to the posts and screwed the pallets into each other. He painted the street-facing side of the fence black and in blood-red paint periodically scrawled blustery notes of warning like "WE DON'T CALL 911" and "NO TRESPASSING: SURVIVORS WILL BE PERSECUTED." That typo is his, I never pointed it out to him.

"My castle. Out there the world might go to shit but inside this perimeter there will always be order and civilization."

"You're the pallet king," I said, kind of joking, being a little bit mean. In some ways it was funny, his fixation with the end of civilization, his belief that he could escape it, but it made me sad. I wished he would just take up golf or something. I mean I more or less believed him that the world was coming to an end but not for the reasons he did and I didn't figure he'd live to see it and he sure as shit wouldn't survive it.

"You know how to run an excavator?" he said. "I'm thinking of digging a moat."

It was all my fault. He didn't have anybody. And it's not like I had anything going on. I was a loser. I couldn't keep a girl, could barely keep a job. Up to my butt in debt because I thought it was a great idea to buy land. I was going to grow switchgrass and turn it into biofuel, get a jump on the future. Shit. Nothing ever works out the way you want it to. I didn't talk to Ben for a few years. It's complicated. Had to do with my mom and things that happened a lifetime ago. After he remarried, which is also after I sort of came back to the church, I started coming back around, but the past was always present with us. We could be friendly but we could never be close. He killed himself because I couldn't perform the most simple Christian act of forgiving him and I couldn't love him enough to keep him alive or to keep him from falling prey to the pathetic band of shit-heels he called his friends. It sounds a bit psych 101 but I see now his second wife being killed the way she was is probably what set him on the path from normal boring dude to pallet king.

I asked him about the guns one time, why he needed so many. He said, "You never know but the way it's going some immigrant is gonna climb over that wall out there and it's gonna be him or me."

I was floored. I'd never heard him say anything hateful like that. I know I should have gotten after him somehow, but I didn't know how and I'm the type of guy that goes straight from zero to ten. You can't make me mad until you finally do and then it's too late. All I said was "No, it's gonna be some paranoid gun nut," and he laughed and said "You're probably right." That "probably right" made me feel like there was some hope for him, like he wasn't really like the racist dingbats he'd hooked up with in his golden years, but of course I was too timid and polite to push him any further.

The more they hung around the less I did. In my head I gave myself a lot of reasons why he could just go fuck himself. He was a grownass man smart enough to know right from wrong and common sense from bullshit and it wasn't my job to teach him. I was just giving myself an out. I've always been a lazy piece of shit. Just a lazy, selfish piece of shit. I could have intervened but I was too wrapped up in my own stupid bullshit to get involved in his stupid bullshit.

I didn't even care enough to give him a funeral. I deserve everything that happened.

The day after the boys showed up I got a visit from the city. They sent a code enforcement officer out to let me know I was going to need to do something about that fence. It was against code. Too tall and an eyesore.

"My dad and I built that fence together."

"Be that as it may, you should have taken the time to consult the city's website or come down to city hall where you would have been provided with a permit and a list of acceptable fencing materials."

"You sound like a robot," I said. I had decided to become the type of guy who says what he thinks. I'd kept my true thoughts to myself for too long and in a way that's what killed my dad.

"Be that as it may," he said, "you have thirty days to remove this fence and get this property cleaned up."

"Or else?"

"Or else we will destroy you, puny human." He had made his voice sound like a robot's. He was making a joke.

I wasted my life. I never did anything. I never stuck with anything. I was just a wanderer who was too lazy to leave home. I always told myself that I still hadn't peaked in life, which meant there were still good things in store, but I was lying. I peaked in high school when I hit a game-winning three in the first round of state. We still got our asses handed to us the next game. That became the theme of my life, getting my ass handed to me.

I was the sixth man on our team, back in the day, which made me the unofficial captain of the B team, the benchwarmers. We were a bunch of fuckups with shitty attitudes and flat jump shots and we called ourselves Team Anarchy. I got an anarchy symbol tattoo on my left bicep just to show it off in games, but it turns out you can't have any visible tattoos when you're playing high school ball so I had to wear a t-shirt under my jersey every game. That stupid tattoo. My mom was like to kill me when she saw it.

It was a few days after the robot came to see me that the boys came back. Uninvited. They had brought liquor. I had taken the week off from work so I was there. I was always there now. I was never going back to work. I was trying to get the place cleaned up so the city wouldn't bulldoze it or whatever they wanted to do but the more I cleaned the more cleaning there was to do. I was flustered. Not in a good head space as some people might put it. I wasn't in the mood to entertain a bunch of playacting conspiracy theorists but they didn't give two shits. Ben deserved a sendoff and they were going to give him one. I kept to myself and gave them their space. I didn't want them there but they outnumbered me and were all carrying. I just kept cleaning. I'd painted "free pallets" on a piece of scrap OSB and I was praying there was someone out there as horny for free pallets as my old man had been. I was dragging spare pallets out to the street and piling them up by the "free pallets" sign when the sheriff pulled up. I was getting real tired of people just popping in.

The sheriff introduced himself, and I introduced myself, and he said "I'm gonna just cut to the chase here. Your pa hadn't been paying his taxes. The taxes on this place is about six years delinquent."

"Oh really."

I didn't really give a shit.

"I'd give your old man a couple warnings but he always blowed me off. Technically the city could take possession of this property right now. But under the circumstances I thought you oughtta have a chance to make it good."

"Make it good."

"You can pay them back taxes and hold on to your pa's estate. Otherwise it goes to the city and they'll put it up for sale."

"Honestly," I told the sheriff, "that would almost be the best thing."

From behind me I heard Monkey say, "Over my dead body."

"This ain't your property, Monkey," said the sheriff. "This ain't your business."

"My ass, sheriff. You've said your piece, now you can get."

"This ain't about me saying my piece. I ain't offering my opinion. I'm saying what is, and I'm giving this young man a chance to save us all the hassle."

"Over my dead body, you hear me?"

"Is your name on the deed, Monkey? Are you offering to give this boy the money to pay the back taxes? He could," he said as an aside to me, "except he's a notorious tightwad." To Monkey, "I'll thank you to keep your opinion to yourself."

"Go fuck yourself, sheriff. Respectfully. I back the blue but all the same you go fuck yourself. You got any idea how much firepower we got in that shop? You'll mind your own business if you know what's good for you."

He grabbed me by the arm and tugged me back inside the fence and he slammed the gate shut. The sheriff hammered on the gate and hollered for us to open it. Monkey told him to shut the fuck up. "Look up, sheriff. You see that glinty thing up on the roof? That's the sun bouncing off the scope of a .50 caliber MRAD. We got a sniper on you, sheriff, and if you don't believe me you just open that gate without our consent and find out."

"You're making a big mistake, Monkey," said the sheriff. "A big one." But he backed away from the gate and went back to his car.

The standoff lasted three days. They shined bright lights at us all night. They played loud music all night and flew helicopters over the shop. The sheriff positioned himself as the negotiator and he'd call Monkey a couple times a day. They could have moved in pretty easy and taken us out. There wasn't anything stopping them. The only hostage was me and as far as the cops were concerned I was one of the bad guys too.

Guns and ammo, liquor and SpaghettiOs and MREs. It was what the old man had spent the last four years of his life preparing for. We had food. We had gallons and gallons of bottled water and five rain barrels. We could last five years if we had to. The boys were using the shrapnel nails to make pressure cooker bombs. Filling empty Fireball bottles with gasoline. Soaking styrofoam in gasoline to make homemade napalm. Cleaning all the guns, making sure every magazine was full of ammo. Monkey was in heaven. The others I could tell were scared, but there was no way out, no undoing this stupid mess. Monkey made it real clear he'd shoot anyone who tried to sneak out or surrender. He wanted to start a civil war. I didn't understand how us getting killed in my dad's shop was going to start a civil war and he didn't make much effort to connect the dots for me.

"This isn't how we might have seen it playing out," he said, "but it's what we've planned for. It's what we've hoped for. Total commitment."

He gave this speech ten times a day. I mostly just sat around and moped about and I did what cleaning I could. Since I couldn't drag any more pallets out to the street I just dragged them to the burn pile and set them on fire. The boys said I shouldn't go outside the shop but they also didn't really care if the cops assassinated me. I wasn't part of the club.

I thought about volunteering for an overnight watch shift and shooting them all in the head while they slept and that was when I knew I had to find a way to end it. On the third day I plopped my bowl of SpaghettiOs on the pallet table so that it would make a very dramatic noise. I shoved my chair back and stood up and said "Y'all this is not what Ben would have wanted."

"Yes it is," said Monkey. "It's exactly what he wanted except he was always too chickenshit to manifest it into being."

"Well it's not what I want."

"We could give two shits."

I took a step toward the door and he raised a gun at me.

"Go ahead you pony-ass wannabe outlaw," I said. "Feel free to shoot me in the back. Otherwise I'm going out there to put a stop to this bullshit."

Except I didn't turn my back to him. He was ready to shoot me. You could see it in his eyes. He wanted to shoot me.

"Just give me a reason, shithead. I'm begging you to give me a reason."

I've sort of been sitting on this information but I have the golden pipes of an angel, and they saved my life that day. Probably the lives of all my dad's dumbass buddies too.

"O say—"

Monkey looked at me, this childlike shocked look, and he said "What are you doing?"

"can you—"

"You little shit," he said over his sniffles, and he lowered the gun. By the time I hit the C on "see" he just lost it. By the time I was at "rocket's red glare" he was in a heap on the floor. Sobbing. Heaving. And I slipped out the front door with my hands so high in the air I could have tickled God's feet.

Naturally we went to jail, but not really for long. About a day. No one was charged with anything that serious. The boys all turned on Monkey and he pled out to a fairly minor charge. He paid a fine and went back to selling lawnmowers. Of course there's no need to even speculate what would have happened to us if we hadn't been a gang of white men.

The sheriff didn't care about us. We did him a favor. Got his face on TV in an election year. Let him feel like a hero. He even got to ride in the chopper. He got a lot of accolades for a quote the papers used in every story they wrote about the incident, where he's reported to have said, "It's important to show restraint. We don't want another Waco." His restraint didn't have fuck all to do with morality or justice or the rule of law. He just wanted my stuff. By the time I got out the cops had the house all locked up. There was caution tape all around and they wouldn't let me in. They gave me my wallet and my phone and my car keys and the rest, they said, was theirs. I got the legal explanation a few days later. The option to pay the back taxes was off the table because the sheriff's department had assumed ownership of the property through a process known as civil asset forfeiture which means if you do a crime the cops get to keep your shit. All those guns. I could've got $10,000 for that arsenal. I could've paid off my credit card. I could've sold the place and paid off my farm. That shop was full of tools, my dad's tools, his dad's old tools. Cops got it all. Maybe I didn't deserve any of it but they sure as shit didn't.

One evening, a week or so, two weeks, it doesn't matter, after they let me out of jail, I was messing around on the tractor, pulling up a couple tree roots, dumping some gravel on the driveway, just sort of festering out there in the wilds, and I got a really bad idea. It was more like the idea got me, like it was out there, just looking for a host, and it found me, and I was just an empty vessel. I undid the front end loader and hooked on the hay spear, then I rode the tractor in to town. I only lived about six miles out. The sheriff's department is right on the edge of town. It was a Sunday night. The place was dead. It looked more like a used-car place that sells cop cruisers than an actual cop shop. I raised the hay spear and drove it straight through the front windshield of a cop car. Not gonna lie, it felt good. I backed out, lowered my implement, and slid the two points of the hay spear under the front of the cop car, then I lifted it up as high as it would go. Unfortunately my little Kubota didn't have the reach to flip a car over from the front so I just reversed and let the cop car slide off and crash into the ground. I moved around and approached another cruiser from the side and flipped that son of a bitch over like it was a toy. I speared the side windows and lifted it up and just banged it up and down on the ground. I did more cars like that. Fucking up the windows, flipping every car I could. Speared some tires. I lifted up a dumpster and dropped it on top of a cruiser. It's all the stuff of legend now. You can watch most of the destruction on the internet from when a passerby started videoing me. The sheriff's department had just gotten a new toy, a big flashy SUV. I speared it and lifted it and crashed it through the front window of the sheriff's office. The sheriff finally showed up a few moments after that and I was still laughing uncontrollably as he shot out my tires, a completely unnecessary move since there was nothing left for me to destroy. He just wanted to use his gun.

They charged me with domestic terrorism because of my stupid anarchy tattoo and gave me twenty-five years. Took twenty-five years away from me, I should say. If I make it out I'll be the same age my old man was when he offed himself. If the world doesn't end first.

Fireworks at Midnight

Mark was always a deep sleeper, slept through many tornado sirens as a kid in Kansas, but as soon as he became a parent he would awaken at the slightest sound, a useful skill when you're living in an imploding civilization. The question now was what could his kids sleep through.

The man in front of him didn't think he'd actually pull the trigger. Mark wasn't sure himself. It took commitment to pull that trigger; you didn't squeeze off a round like with his .22. You really had to pull. The trigger was so heavy because the gun, a .45-caliber SIG Sauer P250, had no safety. It was a good gun, compact, powerful, fit his hand. He'd have liked a bigger magazine, something that held more than eight rounds, although if you need more than eight bullets you're probably in the type of shit that's too deep for a gun to get you out of.

The neighbors probably wouldn't report a shot but you could never really know. The cops had installed acoustic surveillance, which was only supposed to pick up gunshots but in reality was capable of picking up any sounds and most certainly was collecting more than the cops ever let on. You never knew if it was working or not. People kept tampering with the devices and the police kept coming out to repair them. Even when the system worked it was only effective less than a quarter of the time. Not the worst odds, and this motherfucker was really tempting him.

Until this one he'd never wanted to pull the trigger. He still had this infantile notion that he could convert his enemies, so he wanted to hear their stories, find out what motivated them, connect with them, find common ground. He had resentments, too, deep pockets of anger and hatred, but he didn't waste them on scapegoats like immigrants and trans folk. There was something about this one, maybe the exaggeratedly toothy Obama mask he'd been wearing, that made him not give a shit about his background or motivation.

He half-believed we'd have been better off if Trump had won the election. It would have been a circus, the kind of circus where the tightrope snaps and an acrobat breaks his neck and later the lions escape and kill fourteen children before disappearing into the woods, but maybe there wouldn't have been vigilante right-wing death squads roaming the streets in Trump's America. Shit, they would have just gotten jobs with ICE. People were prepared for some increases in whacko militias, but everyone thought the death squads thing was gallows humor, including many of the internet trolls who'd used the hashtag, but the death squads, encouraged by their leader's refusal to concede and his continued claims that the election had been rigged, manifested after the election like a bloodthirsty ghost that's been trapped in an alternate universe for six centuries and accidentally summoned by a group of kids at a slumber party. The new president tried her best to ignore them. She had no qualms about putting immigrant children in cages or dropping bombs on wedding parties in predominantly Muslim countries, but cracking down on violent fascists in her own country was a political risk she wasn't willing to take. Might look like she was targeting her political enemies. Anything she did would be used against her in the next election, and it was easier to do nothing. After the first wave of killings, independent antifascist militias sprang up in targeted neighborhoods like this one.

"I got a family."

"So did that boy you all murdered. I know his family. They're good people. He had a family too."

"Still would if they hadn't snuck into our country to—"

"Shut the fuck up."

He waggled the gun at his hostage, breathed deeply to fight the shaking. He wasn't sure if this white-winger had tracked him down or was here by coincidence. Maybe more were coming. Maybe he should call the police. Maybe this dude was the police. Maybe he could put a bullet through his brain, bury the corpse in the garden, and go back to bed. The only thing that was certain was this fucker would've killed his family, even if he was there by mistake. It wasn't like he would've broken in, wielding two .38s, and been like "Y'all are white? Wrong house, so sorry," and tiptoed politely out.

"You know who I am?"

"Got a pretty good idea."

"You know my name?"

The son of a bitch just smiled at him.

"You look like the dog that caught the car. You don't want to shoot me. I'm not the bad guy. I'm fighting for my family, my country, my heritage. You should be fighting with us."

"I'm fighting with you fuckers."

"You're fighting against us. What're you even doing here? This ain't your hood. Last thing I expected when I saw this shitty house in this shitty hood was a white dude living in it. White guilt? Been there. Over it. There's more to life."

"You picked the wrong house to break into."

"Yeah. I can see that."

Maybe it was fate. He'd never been much for religion but maybe it was God. The toddler had coughed and when Mark went in the room his youngest son was about to fall out of the bed so he brought him into their bed, then looked out the window and saw the guy creeping through the front gate. He grabbed the pistol from the safe, went out the bathroom window, and sneaked around the side of the house to surprise the intruder, a pudgy but muscular white guy hiding behind a mask. He slid back the chamber in a way meant to get attention and coaxed the fucker to the back yard, had him sit in a ratty old lawn chair while he mulled it all over.

"Mind if I smoke?"

He let his silence answer. The commando lit a cigarette and offered one. They called themselves commandos, even had a ranking system that was too convoluted for outsiders to follow. The cigarette could've been a stalling tactic, could've just been a man enjoying his last smoke. Seemed like if more of them were gonna come they'd already be there.

"You read much Martin Luther King? Dr. King says there's three ways to deal with oppression: acquiescence, violence, and—Dr. King's preference— nonviolent resistance. Acquiescence is what you're doing. 'The oppressed,' says Dr. King, 'resign themselves to their doom. They tacitly adjust themselves to oppression, and thereby become conditioned to it.' You look pretty adjusted to life in brown town, brother, but it's a front. Acquiescence doesn't suit you. I can see your fire. That leaves just two methods of resistance: violence and nonviolence. Ask yourself, how far did nonviolence get the blacks? Not far, right? Still living in slums, shooting each other in the streets, accumulating virtually no wealth. I respect Dr. King but he was a dreamer. Pun intended, I guess. Acquiescence, as Dr.

King so rightly put it, 'is the way of the coward.' What he didn't see, right up until he took a bullet, was that nonviolence is the way of the pussy. Nonviolence gets you nowhere. You think we'd be free from England if the founders had believed all this nonviolence bullshit? Sometimes you have to kill to be free. Violence is justifiable if it's used to destroy tyranny and evil. There's only one legitimate method of resistance and that is violence. We are the Resistance, brother, and the things we do, it's not always pretty, but it's necessary. Don't give me that look. We are not racists. We are not bigots. We are not murderers. Those are lies told by the media. We don't hate black people or immigrants or whatever other minority group *du jour* you want to mention but we will not be complicit in our own obliteration. White genocide is real and you might not think of yourself as a perpetrator but you're an enabler. You can shoot me if you want but—"

His five-year-old son was on the floor when he went in to check on him.

"I thought I heard a gun," the boy said. "Why do I have to get on the floor if I hear gunshots?"

"Back in bed, buddy."

He tucked him in, lay down next to him, held his hand.

"Was it gunshots? Why did you tell me I have to get on the floor if I hear gunshots?"

"Don't worry, buddy. It was just fireworks."

That Time I Was a Cop

This guy Nate was convinced I was a cop. Didn't matter what my brother said, he just kept coming back to it. "I know that dude's a cop. This guy a cop?" I hate cops but I didn't care what he thought of me. He was a loser and all I wanted to do was die. I'd been dragged to this shitty garage apartment against my will because I'd been thinking about killing myself and Chris wouldn't let me stay at the house alone and if I couldn't have my way I wasn't going to let Chris have his so I just sat there, silent, nursing my beer on the couch by myself.

Sometimes people would try to talk to me and I wouldn't say shit and they finally all decided to pretend like I wasn't real, or like I was a cum stain on the couch, just an annoyance that was preventing them from sitting down and getting comfortable or playing Wii but that no one was willing to do anything about.

I didn't know Nate. It wasn't his house. No one was even really doing anything that illegal. Someone had been smoking a joint earlier but that's it, so I didn't even know why he cared. There was nothing about me that said cop. I didn't have cop hair or a stupid cop face. I was sloppy and scruffy and slouchy. I was dead on the inside but not in that cop way. I was the least cop-looking dude you could imagine.

The one thing I guess was my pen. I had this pen I carried around. It was made of steel and had this hard nub on one end that was supposed to be hard enough to smash a car windshield like in case you ever drove off a bridge and had to climb out of your car and swim to the surface and didn't have time to roll your window down. As if you would have time to fumble around for and locate your emergency exit pen. I had taken it out of my pocket and was just sort of absentmindedly fucking around with it and it probably did sort of look like a cop pen. Nate kept alluding to it, saying "What the fuck is up with that pen? Why does he even have a pen?"

I hated these guys, I hated this garage apartment. Being in it, with them, it made me want to kill myself even more than usual. So maybe that's what he picked up on. Maybe he had just enough self-awareness to know there was something about him that made people want to kill themselves but not enough to try to figure out what it was and excise it from his personality.

"Yo Chris what's up with this guy. He acts like a cop."

"That's my brother. Like I said. He's in college."

I almost corrected him but I didn't want to break my vow of silence. Chris loved me. He was a good brother. He'd said that bit about me being in college just from force of habit and then he realized it wasn't true, and I could tell he was about to say "Or, well, he was in college, but," and he caught himself. He wouldn't be likely to say anything that reflected badly on me on a normal night, let alone one where he thought I was suicidal. It didn't matter. I still don't think it was fair for them to kick me out of school but who really gives a shit. This world has bigger problems. I sat in the president's office and let him lecture me about academic integrity and I said "I know how much you pay your grad students and adjuncts so suck my dick." It was the coolest thing I've ever said. Probably the only cool thing. All I had done was sell a few essays to help pay for my tuition, I probably could have been reinstated if I'd kept my mouth shut but fuck it.

This was all so long ago.

There was a table in the center of the room where they were all gathered, huddled around it planning out their Taco Bell order as if they were planning a heist. They didn't ask if I wanted anything. Nate went out to get the food even though he was drunk and high and he made it back without killing anyone somehow and the first thing he said was "I see the cop's still here." It was like there was a spell that made these people, everyone but Nate and my brother, not see me or acknowledge my existence, to the point where if Nate talked about me they couldn't even hear him.

They ate their Taco Bell. I sat in my spot. Every now and then I would sneak away to grab a beer. One time I heard someone say "Man where'd all the beer go?" I was a beer ghost.

"D., you ready? D.?" Chris had to help me stand up. I had got hammered. I had just sat there getting hammered at a turtle's pace, never downing anything, just a constant moderate intake.

Nate got in my face one more time, asking me if I was a cop. "Yo man" he said, "what's your problem anyway? If you're a cop you gotta tell me. It's the law."

Chris said I wasn't there to start trouble, to just give me some space, I was having a rough time and I just needed a little space. He said, "Bro his girlfriend just died, just give him a break okay." He tried to whisper it but I heard. I'd asked him not to tell anyone about her.

Nate said "Dude's a fucking cop, I know it. I can't believe you brought a fucking cop here."

Finally I spoke up. I leaned in and made my voice all hard and gravelly, like I was Batman, and said "I know what you did you sick fuck. I'm gonna put you away for a long time."

I had got the idea from a PG Wodehouse book called *Big Money*. Great book. One of the characters goes up to a stranger and says "I know what you did" with the hope that they'd done something bad enough to be scared by him saying that and pay up for his silence. He was lucky enough that the random person he accused was actually a criminal. All I did back then was sit around and read novels. It was kind of nice really. Everything else was bad but that part was nice. Drove Chris crazy because he wanted me to work so I could pay rent but I rather liked being useless and unproductive. Anyway the "you sick fuck" part was an ad lib. I don't think PG Wodehouse would have said that. I shouldn't have said anything, of course. My mom said I was possessed, there was a devil inside me that just took over sometimes and made me say stupid shit. Like telling a paranoid shitbag at a shitty house party I was gonna put him away for a long time.

"You're not gonna do shit," he said. You could tell he wanted to sound calm but he was also kind of shook.

I pulled out my bigass metal pen and waved it in front of his face and said "I've got it all on here. I've got this whole night on video."

I was being facetious, the way I do even though I know better. People don't get it. They never pick up on it.

"Fuck," he said, all worked up. "I fucking knew it. Shit shit fuck."

He started pacing around the living room, pulling at his hair. Honestly I think he was having a panic attack. He muttered "Where's my fucking gun?" and Chris grabbed my shoulder and dragged me out of the house and to his car.

"You shouldn't fuck with people like that," he said after he pulled out of the driveway. He didn't have anything else to say. He just put on a 311 CD and turned the volume up.

Maybe I should feel bad about what happened, what I said, because we found out the next day that Nate killed himself. Chris was pretty pissed about it until it came out the cops had found a ton of porn, the very bad kind, on his computer, so no I don't feel bad. Of all the things I regret, being responsible for the death of a pedo/child molester is not one of them.

What sucks though is after that everyone thought I really was a cop.

Practice Shot

Murph wasn't much off the tee, but his short game was sublime. He knew the angles and he knew how to smack the ball with top spin and more importantly *when* to do it. He'd be stuck in the sand sighting a shot by the top of the flag and you'd think he was going to be two or three strokes just to get safe on the green and he'd lob it out of the pit and land it two or three feet north of the flag with enough English on it to spin it backward where it hit and drop right in the hole. Bob had seen him do it a hundred times and each time it was amazing. He'd ask him how he was able to do that and Murph would say "Honestly I just hate putting." There was no one else with that kind of touch. If the other elements of his game had been as good as his chipping he could've been a pro.

"I'm still thinking of that chip shot for eagle. On number seven. It was like watching Tiger Woods."

"I got a lucky roll," said Murph. "I'm no Tiger."

"Luck my ass," said Bob. "That was some Tiger Woods shit."

Bob leaned back in the truck bed and pulled a beer out of a cooler. He offered one to Murph, but Murph said no. He was always paranoid about drinking before driving. He only liked to drink at home. He was a bit of a stick in the mud in that regard. Bob opened his Bud Light.

"I did a job for this guy the other day who's a member at Timbervale. He said he could get me a tee time next week but it's got to be early in the morning. You think you could sneak away one day?"

Murph didn't look up from changing out of his spikes. He just said no.

"Alright. You change your mind, though, let me know. The thing is I gotta give him enough notice."

"I won't be able to, Bob."

"Okay. Yeah that's fine. I understand. We're still on for the scramble though? Maybe you could ask one of the guys from the office to be on our team. Not that we need them. Between my long game and your chip magic I think we got a real shot at that pot."

"I don't think so, Bob."

"Oh. I already gave them the deposit is all. It's non-refundable. I thought you were in? We were gonna get drinks after." His voice had got shaky. He felt like a stupid teenager asking a girl who was way out of his league to go to prom with him.

Murph stowed his golf bag and spikes and pressed the button to lower his minivan's rear hatch. He looked at his buddy and said "I'm sorry, Bob, I just don't think I can keep doing this."

Bob said, "Doing what, Murph? What are you saying?"

"I don't like sneaking around like this. I don't like lying to Mindy."

"It's just a game of golf. It doesn't hurt anything."

"It would hurt her. If she found out I was still seeing you."

"Christ Murph, you make it sound—"

"I'm sorry buddy."

"You're serious?"

"Like I said, I'm sorry. I wish it didn't have to be this way, but Mindy made it clear. We're taking Katie's side on this. That's just how it is. No hard feelings."

"Jesus, man, what ever happened to bros before hoes."

Bob was sort of joking, but it didn't come across. It was always like that when he tried to make a joke. People were too sensitive.

"You're talking about our wives, Bob."

"I know, I know, it's just."

"I'll see you," said Murph. He didn't even stick out his hand.

Bob's apartment was an apocalypse. He was a depressed teenager who had through some magic he'd never asked for swapped bodies with a grownup, like in the

Tom Hanks movie, except unlike in the dumb movie he never got to swap back. He just lived this way. Never cleaning up after himself. Jerking off furiously night and day. Being inside the apartment made him feel insane. He emptied another can and added it to the collection on the floor. He was out of beer. It was the escape he needed. He walked to the liquor store, not because he was too drunk to drive but just because it was right down the street and walking made him feel like he was at least doing one thing right.

There was all this beer inside, and none of it was for him. The beer was all this fancy yuppie shit, IPAs and amber ales. There was beer that was half coffee and there was beer that tasted like tangerines and there was beer that tasted like chili peppers.

"Whatever happened to just beer?" he said to no one. There were a couple customers plus the dude at the cash register but no one responded. Their failure to engage egged him on. "I remember when beer was just beer. Heck I remember, back in the day, I used to drink a beer that was just called Beer on the label because that's all I could afford." He laughed. If no one else was going to laugh he'd do it himself because it was funny goddamnit. Of course it was the prices that he hated about the array of craft beers before him. He couldn't even really afford the Bud Light.

"Yeah the beer beer's over there," the guy at the counter said. The guy's voice gave away his profound boredom. Bob was becoming a regular and this guy acted like he'd never been in before and his mere presence was offensive. He damn near launched into a tirade about customer service but the whole world was this way now it felt like.

Bob got his Bud Light and felt stupid because there was so much of it and he'd made such a display of himself. He paid for it and left, but he couldn't even wait to get home to crack one open. It was a brazen move nursing a cold one on the sidewalk and it was fine. It tasted good and it felt free and there were no consequences.

Back in the apartment he cracked another beer and he turned on the PS5 he'd bought for his kids, for the every other weekend they were allowed to visit. He had never cared much about video games, never taken any interest in the kids' favorite games, but that was before the body swap. He got sucked into *Hitman 3*, playing it for hours, stopping only for beers and piss breaks. "These graphics," he said to no one, his only companion these days, "they're freaking amazing." It was Saturday night and he was free and single and he should have been getting laid right now. He had read about the things people were doing now, out in the wide, more sexually liberated world. They were licking each other's buttholes. He'd watched people do it on his laptop and his phone and he wanted to try it. He wanted to try it all. Why wouldn't you want to at least try it? She was always saying to the kids how do you know you don't like it if you won't even try it and yet she would never try it. And he was going to die one day, that was what he always came back to. He'd been driving to Home Depot when he saw the crash. Completely avoidable, totally absurd to think that was the way these men had to die. Two guys who were so determined to make left turns where neither one was allowed to make a left, and they crashed into each other and died. He saw it all happen, he could see it about to happen and he said "No, don't," but it didn't matter. Really fucked him up. He almost got caught up in it, but he was able to swerve around them just in time. The crash is what started it. The crash is what broke them up. They just had different desires. He didn't think of himself as a man with needs, whose needs weren't being met. He wasn't owed anything. He was just a man with a finite amount of time, and he and Katie seemed to want to spend their time, what time they had left, differently. If she didn't want to try these things, have these experiences, that was her right, but wasn't it his right to go out and try it on his own? It was all very reasonable, at least in his mind. Around midnight his neighbor banged on the wall and shouted for him to shut the fuck up. Bob was livid, but he'd seen the neighbor and didn't want anything to do with him. He turned off the game and went to bed. Alone as usual. He wasn't even trying anymore.

Somewhere in his sleep Bob dreamed that he was walking in the desert, looking for the end of the world because when he got there he would have to kill The

Leader and then he'd have his answer. He'd have all the answers. When he got there all he saw was a giant toilet. He walked over and stood on the rim of the toilet, looked down into the nothingness. He thought about jumping into the toilet abyss, but instead he just peed. Pulled it out and let it fly, whipped it around like he was putting out a fire. When he woke up the sheets were soaked.

Katie had got everything. She got the house. She got the kids. She got the dog. She got the good car. She got their friends. She knew how hard it was for him to make friends. Murph was the only one he had. He hadn't even done anything. He never cheated. He was good to her and the kids. But there were things that he wanted. He wasn't satisfied. He still sort of loved her, but the idea of spending the rest of his life with her had made him want to die. He would think to himself how for the rest of his life he would never be with another woman, and the older they got the less sex there would be, and one day he'd find he couldn't even get it up, and one day after that he'd die, and he'd be overcome with dread. Maybe if she died first he'd have a chance but what kind of way was that to think? All this was embarrassing enough to admit to himself and he had no idea how to translate it for anyone else, make it make sense to them. He sounded so pathetic. "Time is infinite," he had once said to Murph, who hadn't asked, "but our time is finite. Finite. This is all we get and if you don't shoot your shot you don't get another one. I have to shoot my shot."

"Just so I'm clear, you're talking about fucking right now?"

"What? No. I mean, yes, but not just. It's more than that. It's more than fucking."

"Well," Bob had said. "Speaking of shots. You're up buddy and we've got a foursome on our ass. Go ahead and shoot your shot."

In his ideal life on this morning he should have been waking up early not to change some piss-soaked sheets but to make breakfast for a woman he'd only met the night before. But there was never any woman, no matter what he did, what he said, how he dressed, how many drinks he sent over. The thing is when you're a basically middle-aged single dude with just sort of a medium job and a fifteen-year-old pickup truck and you don't have some sort of very sympathetic reason (your wife left you for your brother, your wife was killed in a mass shooting) for being single there is pretty much no one who wants to fuck you. It was the cruelty of fate. It was life. It was fucking bullshit.

He saw on Facebook that Mindy and Murph were having a barbecue next weekend, which should have been the weekend of the scramble. The food would be mediocre and the guests would be boring and there was nothing he wanted more than to be welcome at this stupid barbecue. He threw his phone at the wall but it still worked. He pulled his driver out of his bag and brought the oversized head down on his phone. He propped the phone on top of the TV remote and took a full swing, driving a beauty right into the wall he shared with his angry, beefy neighbor. He hurried out the door and got in the truck and peeled out of the pathetic parking lot of his pathetic apartment complex. It was Sunday morning and he should have been on the golf course.

He got to the house, to Katie's house, technically, and didn't really know what to do. He just sat in the truck for a few minutes, thinking, sweating, hyperventilating, but the kids saw him and Katie came out to find out what the fuck he wanted. What he wanted, he finally told her, improvising, letting his mouth make up his mind for him, was a mulligan. "A do-over," he told her. "To pretend like this never happened. To erase this from our lives. It was all just a practice shot. Can we do that? Is that a possibility?"

He reeked of urine and his eyes were filled with fear, as if they were staring in horror at a dangerous animal behind her, or a maniac with a big gun, but there was nothing behind her. Only the house. Only their life.

"What?" she said. "Bobby I can't understand you, you're blubbering. What are you doing here? What do you want?"

"A mulligan," he said.

"What? You're not speaking clearly."

"A mulligan," he said. "A mulligan," he shouted. He banged his head against the steering wheel, seven or eight times, saying "A mulligan a mulligan a mulligan a mulligan."

"To be born again? Is that what you said baby? Is that what you want?"

And he said "Yes that's it."

The next weekend he went to the barbecue like nothing ever happened.

Timewarp

"My boyfriend says you're in love with me."

"What? No. That's absurd," I said. All cool. "Just absurd. I mean."

I wanted to die. Like if there was a way to just be clicked off like a TV, and maybe clicked back on when she was gone, that's what I wanted. I was so convincing in not being in love with her that she started to get offended.

"I just remember you used to sort of have a thing for me, and I just wanted to be up front that I don't feel that way about you."

"That's fine," I said. "That's good. Because I don't feel that way either. About you. Just absurd."

"I just would hate to think you were doing this because, like…"

"No. No no. Of course not. I'm doing this because I believe in you, I mean in your idea."

I pulled a check out of my pocket and handed it over and I said, "This is how much I believe in this business."

She smiled. I could have died.

"That was awkward," she said. "Sorry I made it awkward."

"Wasn't awkward. Don't be silly. We're both adults."

I didn't feel like one.

She cashed the check that same day.

. . .

I had to get a second job. I was doing okay finally. I had my own house now and no mortgage. My car was paid off. All I had was student loans and utility bills. Her boyfriend was right though. It was weird to be almost forty, living back in my hometown, in love with the same girl again. I had gone through a timewarp.

We'd hooked up at a funeral. Not hooked up like went to bed together, just hooked up like "Oh wow I didn't know you still lived here. We should like get together sometime." So we had coffee. And we had lunch. And she asked me if I could pet-sit for her while she and her stupidass boyfriend went to the Gulf for the week and I said of course. And she told me her dream was to open a video store that only carried 80s movies and I said that's an awesome idea because people still love *Karate Kid* and there's so much 80s nostalgia out there, plus people just miss video stores, I fucking love video stores, and she asked if I could invest and I said of course. She was needlessly limiting herself by focusing solely on 80s movies, there was a ton of nostalgia for plenty of other decades out there, and honestly we're not that far off from *Donnie Darko* and *Superbad* being regarded as classic films, but I didn't want to sabotage whatever slim chance I had with her by pointing out an obvious flaw in her business plan.

The way I saw it, she might not love me back if I invested in her business, but she definitely would not love me back if I turned her down. So I gave her $20,000. What I did was I opened up a line of credit, transferred the balance to my checking, and wrote her a fat check.

It was a bad business idea. It was never going to work. She had no real business plan, which is why the bank wouldn't give her anything, but the Family Video was going out of business and she had her eye on the building. It was an ugly building but people were used to there being a video store there so she felt the timing was right. Circle of life. A phoenix rising from the ashes except this time being a lot cooler, no offense to Family Video.

I would have said yes to anything. If Julia had said "I want to start a revolution. I want to slaughter our enemies and burn down the White House," I would have given her $20,000 for arms and ammunition.

I was working in a donut shop. I got that job the way everyone in this town gets a job, by knowing someone, specifically the owner, this guy named Roger. Huge piece of shit. Complete scumbag. But he gave me a job because he wanted to fuck my sister. My sister was his Julia and it occurs to me now, it makes me shudder, that maybe I'm someone's Roger. I mean I'll never be able to hook someone up with a job but what if all I am to some people is just some dude with no value to the world other than an existential desire to fuck Julia? I want to do so much more than fuck her, but that sounds bad and it's also beside the point. Anyway the pay was shit but the donuts were free and the work was easy enough, aside from how early I had to wake up.

I had taught fourth grade English for more than ten years at a public school in Chicago. I loved it. I loved living there. Loved my job. I was happy. I was fulfilled. I was always broke. I applied here, figured with my experience I'd get something pretty quick, but the principal at the first school I applied to called me after the interview and said "Look you're the most qualified candidate we've had in years but the truth is we looked at your Facebook and saw the picture of you at the Black Lives Matter thing."

"Yeah," I said, "okay."

"Look, bud, you seem like a nice guy but I can tell you the parents here would not look too kind if we hired a teacher who consorts with terrorists."

"You're not fucking serious."

"Out of my hands."

So instead of hiring me they hired a guy who I saw on the news a few months later was a child molester. I called my sister but none of the guys who wanted to fuck her worked in a school. But did I remember that jerkoff Roger?

The shop was called The Donut House. It was a themed donut shop, with the title doing a little too much work, being a play on "the nut house," as in insane asylum, which I always had to explain to people. Once they got it they ate it up. We didn't have regular donuts like long johns and bearclaws, or we had regular donuts but they all had stupid names that fit the asylum theme. You didn't order a bearclaw, you ordered a straight jacket. You didn't order a chocolate-frosted with sprinkles, you ordered a chocolate frosted with happy pills. The workers all wore white uniforms, but like what the orderlies wore in *One Flew Over the Cuckoo's Nest*, not normal bakery uniforms. It was demeaning and offensive and people loved it.

The money was terrible and nobody tipped. But it was enough to survive. To barely pay the bills. I figured I could coast like that until another guy with a hardon for my sister could hook me up with something better. Then my hardon for Julia got me into debt.

I couldn't find anything, not that I looked super hard. Part of me didn't care about the money. The only reason I gave a shit about paying it back was I knew if I didn't the bank would take the house. Plus her boyfriend may have been a worthless sack of shit but Julia wasn't likely to trade down for a dude who had his inherited house repossessed.

I moved home for the same reason everyone does, I didn't have anywhere else to go. My landlord wouldn't let me renew my lease without a rent hike and I couldn't afford the rent she was demanding. She said, "I feel for you, I really do." And I said, "Oh you feel for me? Okay. Yeah that makes it better. That makes it okay. I feel better now. Truly." She said, "You know your tone is very aggressive and very triggering to me. Sarcasm is such a pathetic cishet white male defense against vulnerability. It's cliché, but it's also very harmful and violent. You should think about the harm you do other people."

When my mother died in an ear candle mishap a few weeks later my sister said "What should we do with the house?" and I said "Shit, can I just live in it?" And there you go. I had no permanent attachments to Chicago, just my job and a few friends, no kids, no wife or girlfriend or vague long-shot love interest, just a handful of exes, none of whom were likely to be heartbroken anew at the thought of me disappearing. Dad had died a few years earlier in a mass shooting at a gender reveal party. We were estranged by then but I was still fucked up by it.

I really did go through a timewarp. As I got within forty miles of my town I lost the signal on the classic rock channel I was listening to and I started scanning, and the first thing that came up was 99.9 *Na-Na-Na-Na 90s* and the song that was playing was "Cumbersome" by Seven Mary Three, a song I probably hadn't heard in all the years I'd been gone. Every party, every road trip, every shuffle of my iTunes library, presented an opportunity, yet the gods never queued it up. But back home, for all these years, it's been on the daily rotation. "Your life has become cumbersome," the dude from Seven Mary Three sang, and I was like, fuck.

The internet is slower here. Business is slower here. Julia's bank was afraid to cash my check because it was from a bank in Chicago. I had to call up the manager at her bank and plead with him to clear it. "I feel for you, buddy," he told me, "but it's out of my hands. It's been flagged by the fraud division so it's out of my hands."

"They can't call up my bank? The funds are in there. You're telling me there's no way for your bank to verify those funds are in there? You guys can't just pick up the phone and call my bank?"

"Like I said, it's out of my hands."

"What if you just cancel the check and we do a wire transfer?"

"Hmmm, I'm not sure. I know we have a way for customers to transfer money out but I don't know if they can receive it. I'd have to check the website. Of course the website's down so that'll take a couple days."

"I thought I was talking to the manager."

"Well what you've got to understand is there's a lot of ins and outs."

"Are we living in the fucking 80s? Just clear the check so my partner, my business partner I mean, not like my *partner* partner, can start her business. I'm trying to conduct business and you're standing in our way. Do you not like business?"

In the end I just had to wait, Julia just had to wait, which killed me, but it cleared. Three days later. "I knew it would," she said, like she was so proud of me.

I finally remembered this app, WRENCHR, that I'd heard about in Chicago. You buy a new bookshelf or bed frame and then realize you're an incompetent degenerate and don't know how to put it together, you go on the app and somehow it connects you with someone who's smart enough to read IKEA instructions but not smart enough to do anything good with their life. So I signed up. Armed with a cell phone and a couple Allen wrenches, I began a career as a freelance furniture assembler. It was about as lucrative as it sounds. There was no hourly rate, people just posted what they were willing to pay and you could bid for the gig or not. There was an option to tip but no one ever did. This is a part of the country where people are very opposed to both the tipping economy and the paying-people-a-fair-wage economy. Which is why they call it Real America.

Occasionally I'd find myself in the home of someone who knew me back when. It was always awkward. I should have had a higher-status occupation. I'd say I was trying to gin up a little extra cash to buy a boat or add on to my house. There was a woman I'd gone to school with, Cara, we had actually gone to prom together. It looked like she'd just moved in. Like this wasn't where she wanted to be. Like me. So I said, "I probably shouldn't say anything, but I could build you a book case that was sturdier than this one and way more attractive for pretty much what you paid for this. Just something to think about."

She said, "You're right, you shouldn't have said anything."

Men were the worst. I put together a lot of bunk beds for divorced dads. They all felt like they should have been doing this stuff for themselves and they always had excuses, like they just didn't have time or they'd thrown out their back at the gym. Married dads were the worst. They all knew better than me how to put this shit together. I couldn't tell them to do it themselves since they were the experts because then they'd one-star me on the app and I'd get fewer clients. It doesn't feel right calling them clients. Clients are for lawyers and drug dealers but that's what the online training called them.

. . .

My phone buzzed. I expected it to be some incompetent he-man looking for a loser like me to mount his new TV, but it was Julia. She never texted me at night. I nearly died getting over to her place. Not one but two cars completely ran red lights. Didn't slow down, didn't respond to my blaring horn or torrent of curse words. My light turned green and I was about to go and this guy in a blue Ford Explorer just blazed right through. If I hadn't noticed him he would have killed me. I stopped to buy a bottle of wine and then it happened again two blocks down the road, this time with a Dodge Caravan. You really have to wait three seconds before you go off a green light in this town, and just ignore the honking from the shithead behind you who's really eager to watch you die. I was amped up when I got to her house and my voice was strained from screaming. It made me kind of rude. "What the fuck is wrong with these people?" I said when she opened the door. "Who drives like this? I brought wine, I hope you like red," handing it over. "Nobody drives like this anywhere. Every time I get in the car I'm nearly killed. Twice on the way over here. I remember people being bad drivers here but this is something else. People drive like they don't value their lives, and I guess I can't blame them. It's like living in a bad science fiction movie where aliens are taking over people's bodies and they don't know how to drive."

"That doesn't make sense, though, because if they can fly a spaceship wouldn't they be able to drive a car?"

You can see why I loved her. I wanted to kiss her, tell her I loved her. God, she was sexy. She'd always been conventionally incredibly fucking hot but there was something ineffable about her as well, otherworldly, divine, I don't know, I'm not a scientist. It blew me away, the effect she still had on me. If she was an alien trying to take control of my body I didn't give a fuck.

"Anyway," she said, "have you seen that new car wash on 32nd?"

"There's like thirty car washes on 32nd. Car washes are like Starbucks in this town."

"Yeah but it's the new one. It's called Blood of the Lamb Wash 'N' Wax. People go there and their car is washed in the blood of the lamb of God and that's supposed to protect them. There's always a long line."

I apologized for coming in hot, asked her what was going on.

"You're probably gonna hate me," she said.

"I doubt that." Impossible. I wasn't in control of my feelings for her. It was out of my hands.

"It's just, Jerred's out of town. He's got his kids this weekend and he goes and stays at his dad's when he has his kids I think because his ex doesn't want them around me because I'm such a slut or whatever but also I think he just likes having his dad around so he doesn't have to deal with the kids the whole time, you know, and well I got this new TV…"

"Oh. Yeah, of course. I'll just grab my tools."

It took me all of seven minutes to get the TV mounted. I was a pro. I programmed the remote for her, as well, and got her signed in to Netflix. I eyeballed the wine, unopened on the coffee table. She picked it up, all casual, and said "This was sweet. I better save it for later though. I had a," yawning, "long day."

I took the hint and of course I nearly died on the way home. Rear-ended by an F-150. Jammed me right up into the rear of the F-150 in front of me, accordianing my little Civic. I had to kick out the windshield. No one even tried to help me climb out. There was blood all over my head. The driver ran up to me. He didn't say he was sorry or ask if I was okay. He just got down on his knees and said, not to me but to humanity, "Don't you see, this proves it. I wasn't even wearing my seat belt. I should be dead right now, but my truck has been washed in the blood of the lamb."

I only had liability and he had no insurance at all. Jesus was his insurance.

...

The Civic was ruined, unsalvageable, but I had to have a car. I took all the money I'd made from my side gig so far and made a payment on the line of credit. Then I upped the line of credit enough to let me buy and get repaired my neighbor's 1998 Dodge Neon. Time was the road belonged to the Dodge Neon. Just a little window where you'd be driving down the road and every other pair of headlights was angled back in such as a way as to be looking down at you for not driving a Dodge Neon. Technically I could have walked to the donut shop, or bought a used bike, and either of those would have been better for me, albeit only theoretically: if I'd tried it I'd have been killed, either run over or shot dead, likely as not both. There's incredible truth in the old saw about how you've got to spend money to make money, but most of the time you end up spending more than you make, especially if your hustle is assembling furniture.

I got called in for a sofa emergency. This guy had ordered it from IKEA and didn't know it was going to come in a box. IKEA calls were rare because the closest one was two and a half hours away. Still some people made the trek. When I got to the house the door was opened by a man with the biggest teeth I've ever seen. They weren't sharp, just big. He had a long, narrow horse face and large, flat horse teeth. I wanted to feed him an apple.

The couch took me about thirty minutes to assemble. The only hard part was putting the cover on the cushions. The guy was impressed. He watched me the whole time and would occasionally nod as if I was his student and he was proud of me for mastering a concept he'd spent a lot of time trying to get through my thick head. Other times he would say "Ahhhhhhhhh" as if he was the one with the thick head and I'd revealed to him some ancient secret.

When I was done he said, "Brother, follow me. I'm gonna show you something that'll change your life."

I followed just on the off-chance the something was a decent tip, which of course it wasn't. He took me into his kitchen and pointed at a blender. There was a tub of what looked like protein powder next to the blender. The guy stood on the other side of the island and it felt like I was inside an infomercial.

"Have you heard of this stuff?"

"No," I said. It was called Mustang Milk.

"It's called Mustang Milk. It'll change your life."

"Ahhhhhh."

"You've probably seen other protein powders or nutritional supplements," he said. "Maybe you've even tried some."

I nodded my head. He was right.

"But I promise you've never tried anything like this. It's got everything. It's packed with complete protein. Aminos. Minerals. Antioxidants. It's whole-istic. It treats your whole body, not just your muscles. It's got fuel for your body *and* fuel for your brain. That's what makes it different."

I held up my phone. "Seems cool," I said, "but I got another gig I need to get to."

"Sure sure sure, just one second. I'll make you one for the road."

"That's not necessary."

"The thing about this stuff is it's got two key ingredients you won't find in any other supplement. Some people get freaked out at this part but it's these two key ingredients that set Mustang Milk apart from every other supplement."

I stayed put. I was listening politely. Okay at this point I was dying to know the ingredients.

He turned the tub around, facing the ingredients list, which I was too far away to read, toward me.

"Hear me out, I'm just gonna say it: it's horse semen and horse brains. That's the ticket."

"Yeah man I'll check it out. Gotta get going though. Thanks bro."

"It sounds weird, I know, but there's a crisis of masculinity in this country and this stuff is the answer. I'm serious. It's not gay, it's not from dudes. Honestly it would be better if it was human semen but there's a legal gray area around the legality of that. A lot of red tape due to quote-unquote AIDS so the company decided it would be best to go with horse semen. Plus there's the logistical issue of where would we get all the human semen, what with masturbation being immoral and wasteful, and it would end up being too costly, meanwhile there's a glut of horse semen on the market. You can get it for pennies on the dollar. But buddy it's that semen that gives you the virility you need, the stamina, and it's a complete protein. It's a superfood, even more so than chia seeds and açai berries. In fact the reason that women and gays have such an advantage in Western society these days is because they ingest so much semen. It makes them smarter and guys like you and me, we've got to catch up. There's also powdered horse brains, and if you think about it, I mean, yuck, but also if you think about it it totally makes sense. Total brain power. Horses are one of the smartest animals, huge brains. Huge peckers too. I'm just saying."

"Yeah dude, thanks."

"It's also got whey, creatine, and extra testosterone."

"Sounds awesome, really, but I need to head."

"Wait, let me show you the trick, my little special finishing touch." I wished he hadn't said either "finishing" or "touch." He poured something out of a little vial into the blender. "Little CBD oil, takes it to the next level. I've actually been trying to get in touch with the CEO of Mustang Milk to try to get them to produce a CBD version."

He added a little milk, closed the lid, and turned on the blender, which was my cue to leave, but he cut the blender.

"Hang on, it'll just take a second and I'll put some in a to-go cup for you."

"Thanks, man, honestly, but it's policy. I'd love to try it but I'm not allowed to accept gifts from clients." I was lying.

"Dude, you don't need this shit job anymore. Fuck it, bro. I'm gonna let you in on a little secret: I sell this shit, I sell mad amounts of it and I'm looking for a partner. I was watching you work tonight and you have a good head on your shoulders and a good work ethic. I want you as my partner."

"Sorry man, I'm just an assembler. That's what I'm good at. I don't know how to sell brain juice."

He turned the blender back on and I went for the door. I started the engine without even putting on my seatbelt but before I could back out of the driveway he was there with a brain-jizz smoothie in a red Solo cup for me. He was begging me to try his smoothie, said he'd put everything he had into it, and then he realized how that sounded and he said "My life savings, my whole life savings. I cashed everything to invest. I need this, bro, I mean it's a sure thing."

I said, "Trust me, dude, I know how you feel," and I backed out and he ran after me. I shifted into first, squealing my tires, and he squealed above them, "There's a crisis in masculinity, man, a crisis in masculinity!"

In the rearview I watched him down that smoothie. When I got home I saw that he one-starred me.

...

There was another app, an app for people with no moral center. You log on and the app shows you where there are people who are behind on their car payments near you, and you can show up at their home or place of business to bully them. You're not supposed to kill anyone because that creates a legal headache for the company but the couple times it's happened the killers were acquitted and got to keep what was left over from the GoFundMes their supporters set up to pay their legal fees, which seeing as the company paid for the lawyers turned out to be a substantial payday. Even if you don't assassinate anyone this app pays way better than WRENCHR. Got a cooler name, too: DebtSquad.

One of these goons showed up at my house. He was waiting on my doorstep when I got home from The Donut House one day.

"Took you long enough," he said. "I've been waiting here seven minutes."

"Do I know you?"

"No. But I know you. I know you stopped for gas on the way home from work, I can see it all right here," holding up his phone, which was full of my private information, "and I know you went inside the gas station and bought a fountain drink you can't afford, seeing how you still owe JPMorgan Chase Bank 20K not even to mention buttloads upon buttloads of accrued interest."

"I didn't know banks made house calls."

"Let me tell you, brother, I ain't the bank. I'm the son of a bitch the bank calls to do the work they don't want to do themselves."

The debt collector, a white guy in his fifties, had a white goatee and dark wraparound sunglasses, bandana on his head like a knockoff Stevie Van Zandt. He had on a black cutoff t-shirt with a skull on it with the slogan "Work sets you free." It was hard to get a read on whether he was a guy who just liked that phrase without knowing its history or whether he liked it because of its history. He was probably in his fifties and looked like he worked out in spurts. I figured I could take him if it came down to it but he had an evil vibe that would make him hard to take down.

He stood up and handed me a collections letter. Another one for my personal collection.

"Found this in your mailbox," he said.

"That's a federal crime," I said, and he laughed.

"Today's visit was a warning." He pulled out a cigar and a cigar cutter to snip off the end. He made a big show of it. He made a big show of lighting it. And he made a big show of taking a big first puff. When the show was over he handed me the cut tip of the cigar and said, "Next time I get to take home a souvenir."

He drove a gray Nissan Cube and it was parked in front of my house. When he drove away I got back in my car and drove to the closest gun shop and used my Chase card to buy a rifle and two pistols. I was mainly sending a message, let them see those purchases and think hard about how they wanted to approach me for repayment.

. . .

That night I got called to an empty house. This town was full of empty houses. It had an eerie feel, but the owners of these empty houses were the only ones around here with any sense. I put together a desk and a bed frame and a closet organizing system. I had to take pictures of each item and upload them to the app in order to prove I'd done the work. It was the best-paying gig I'd picked up. More gigs like this and I'd stand a chance. I saw a little entry book in the front hallway, filled with testimonials of people who had spent the night in this house, and I realized it was an Airbnb. There were long gaps between the dates of the entries because who the fuck would want to come here. I walked out of that house, locked the door behind me, replaced the key in the secret key spot, and looked around at all the empty houses on the street. I spotted at least four. I could tell because everyone here just leaves their trashcans out on the sidewalk throughout the week and the sidewalks in front of those four houses were clear and maneuverable, the only ADA-compliant sidewalks on the block. No lights on inside. No cars in the driveways. There had to be shit inside to rob though.

I met up with a couple old friends at a steak joint called The Main House. I'd driven past it before without thinking much of it, other than it must be called that because it's on Main Street. But no. Of course no. Nothing is ever what you think it is and it's always so much worse than you thought. It was a plantation-themed steakhouse. All the waiters were white people in blackface. I was sitting there drinking a Bud Lime in a frosty mug when it really sunk in. I'd been distracted by my nascent robbery scheme when I first came in and we were seated at our table.

"What the fuck is this place?"

I was there with Deb and Chuck. This was the first time we'd got together since I'd moved back. I hadn't seen them in probably seventeen years. I didn't know they were like this now, they certainly didn't used to be, is what I'm saying.

"You guys want apps?" said Deb.

"What is happening?"

"I could go for some tater skins," said Chuck.

"Why would you bring me here?"

"Relax," said Deb.

"Don't be so sensitive Professor Woke-man," said Chuck.

The waiter came over, plastic chains wrapped around his ankles making him drag his feet.

He looked at me and, without shame or embarrassment, with just pure demented normalcy, said, "Can I take ya order massuh?"

Generally I would say solidarity with all service industry workers, but not this Mark Twain novel motherfucker. I threw my beer in his face, something I'd never done before nor ever really pictured myself doing, and he stumbled back and his feet got caught in the chains and he tripped and crashed into a busboy carrying a tub of dirty dishes that crashed onto the table next to ours. One of the guys from that table got up and threw a punch at me. I ducked it and launched myself into him with a good solid shoulder tackle. I had the force and momentum to lift him off the ground and I dropped his ass right on top of his table. Broke it and fucked him up good. He got a concussion and sliced his ass open on a smashed soup bowl. People were screeching and death loomed over the place. It could have got real bad. I was dragged out of the restaurant and a bunch of people got cheap shots in but everyone who did came out looking worse than I did. My hands ended up covered in other people's blood. Also ketchup from when I landed a punch on a messy eater's jaw. I wanted to kill every motherfucker in that place. It was good, yet in another sense too bad, I hadn't picked up my guns yet.

Every restaurant in this town that didn't already exist when I was born had a theme. You could get burgers at The Cop Shop, Where Cops Eat Free, and where the waiters all have real guns and fake badges. They write your order down on a traffic ticket that they leave on the table because they call it in over a walkie. At Hunter's Green there are game animals just wandering around outside and for an extra $50 the waiter will hand you a bow and let you shoot your dinner. They say that but what you end up with is meat from a deer someone killed last week, and of course no one really likes venison or actually getting their hands dirty so most people order beef, which is imported from Brazil. The most popular restaurant in town is Border Run, which is part of a chain owned by the GEO Group. All the kitchen staff are ICE detainees awaiting deportation. People go wild for their queso.

When I think of all the towns the Union soldiers burned down in this region I am reminded that they didn't burn down enough of them.

I called my sister later, to see if she knew any lawyers (she did, no hornier profession than lawyering), just in case anyone had called the police and got my license plate, and I said "What is the deal with all these theme restaurants?"

"I don't know. It's fun. People like it. Makes them feel like they're in a different world."

"Well all I want is a theme restaurant where not everyone is insane."

"Yeah good luck with that."

. . .

"Why was the comedian always going to the hardware store?"

"I don't know. Wait is this a joke?"

"Yes."

"Oh cool, uh, I don't know, why *was* the comedian always going to the hardware store?"

"Because you can never have too many bits."

She laughed. My drill bit had just broken and I'd asked her to grab me the box of bits and it had taken a lot of explaining, would have been faster to drop what I was doing and go grab it. Of course then I wouldn't have had time to think of that joke.

She had called me up a couple weeks prior and asked if I knew how to build a deck because she wanted to put a deck in her back yard and some guy had quoted her $12,000.

"Yeah of course," I said. It was a lie. "Matter of fact I'm just getting ready to build a deck here at my place. If you want, when I'm done, I can build one for you. No cost. Just the materials." She couldn't pass that up. Honestly if she had hesitated even slightly I was prepared to tell her I had ordered too much lumber and she could have my overage.

"Where did you learn to do this?" she asked me, impressed with the string line I'd put up to keep our corners square and guide us on our level.

"Here and there," I said. "Some odd jobs in college. Little from my old man."

Lies. It was all *YouTube*. My old man never taught me anything. When I was in Boy Scouts my mom helped me build a race car for the pinewood derby. We didn't put that much effort into it, I think we just bought it as a package at the hobby shop and plopped it together and stuck the stickers on. I knew, realistically, I didn't have a shot, but as I descended the steps to the St. Mary's Church basement I felt like maybe I did have a shot, like my car could win. What better setting for a miracle. I watched the other boys race their cars. Their cars looked sleeker, heavier. Mine looked like a piece of wood with stickers on it. There was no way my car would go as fast as theirs. My only hope was to come up against another kid with divorced parents. I don't remember who I drew. I don't remember who was there. When it was my turn to race I put my car on the track and when I let it go it didn't even move. Julia had a way of making me feel just like that car.

So right away I opened a Home Depot credit card and put a bunch of tools on it, a chop saw, a good impact driver, a builder's level and tripod, a shitload of deck screws and lumber, and bits, buttloads of bits, and spent all my free hours learning everything there was to know about deck building. Then hours of trial and error, mostly error, in my back yard, building a deck I hadn't actually wanted. Turned out okay. When I was done I went back and put a really nice grill on my Home Depot card. It's a sweet place to cookout and every time I made burgers or kebabs I'd smile and remember how much money I owed on that fucking credit card.

Julia's deck took three full weekends to complete. Three full weekends we got to spend together, just me and Julia. Jerred didn't lift a finger. Didn't drive a single screw or lug a single bag of concrete. The most he contributed was every once in a while he'd walk by with a cold beer and say "Looks like you're working hard."

It felt amazing, to see this deck completed. We had built it together, without bickering or falling out. That's not an easy thing. You have to be simpatico.

When we'd placed the last board she popped us both a beer and she sat on the edge of the deck with her feet dangling down. I moved up close to get my beer and I didn't move away. She smiled and said "Finished."

"What about a railing?" I was concerned for her safety and I didn't want it to end.

"Eh. No one's gonna fall off. If whoever buys this house one day has kids they can add a rail. I'm not gonna need it."

"Really?"

She nodded toward the house, the air-conditioned house where Jerred was splayed out on the couch playing video games. "You think I'm gonna start a family with that joker?"

It was the most beautiful thing anyone had ever said.

Where we were, her sitting on the deck and me standing in the grass, we were the perfect height to kiss. All I had to do was lean in. It was the perfect height for us to lock lips, for her to lock her legs around me and squeeze me tight and wrap her fingers in my shaggy hair. The perfect height for me to slide my hand up the backside of her shirt and undo her bra, then watch her eyes to see if it was okay for me to lift her shirt. The perfect height for her to moan while I sucked on her tits. The perfect height for her to lie back and raise her butt to let me slide off her little running shorts and panties, the perfect height for her to writhe and moan while I ate her pussy and—sorry, got carried away. Hang on.

It was the perfect height for me to kiss her but I didn't lean in. I didn't make a move. I've never known how to make a move.

...

I picked up a shelf gig at a house in a gated neighborhood on the outskirts of town. Where when I was a kid there was just boundless woods there was now tidy green grass and paved roads and shitty expensive houses. Barf.

It was a floating shelf, you just mounted the frame to the wall studs and slid the faux-oak shelf over it and fixed it with a couple pocket screws. Easy. Something he should have been able to do so naturally he had to justify why he wasn't doing it.

"I've worked my whole life," he said. "You get to my age it's time to pay someone else to do this stuff."

"I saw that big truck in the driveway. You work in construction or something?"

A spotless white quadcab Dodge Ram with a Cummins diesel and big old off-road tires. Set him back at least $60,000. I wanted to steal it. You've heard the old question of can God make a rock that's too heavy for him to move? The jury may be out on God but that truck could still tow it.

"Radio. Sales rep."

The true working class.

"Hey what's that yard sign about? If you don't mind my asking."

It had a big red NO on the left, taking up all the height of the sign. Next to the NO in smaller type it said "Noise Pollution," "Nanny State," and "Sirens" stacked in a column. The big red NO was a no to all these things.

"Oh they want to expand the tornado siren system to out here and I don't want no part of it."

"You don't hear the sirens out here?"

"Not yet. And we want to keep it that way. Most of us moved out here to get away from the tornado sirens."

"I guess I don't understand."

"Tornado sirens is Big Government nanny-statism and Real Americans pay them no heed."

"But what if you're asleep?"

"Exactly."

"A siren could save your life."

"I don't want my tax money going to that."

"I see."

He set a picture of Jesus on the shelf and stood there and stared at it. Then he said "There's all the tornado siren I need."

"No offense, but my aunt and uncle and two cousins were killed in a tornado in '97 and if the siren system had been better then they might still be here.

Their cute little dog too. Not that the dog would still be here."

"Buddy if you believe that there ain't nothing I can say to convince you. All I can say is they'll install sirens in Crystal Meadows over my dead body."

He paid me $5 with no tip. Gave me three stars. I had to drive on the grass to get out of the compound because the gate wouldn't open.

...

"What's your favorite 80s movie?"

"Oh my god," she said. "It's funny. I haven't even thought about that. I should have one."

"People will ask."

We were out on her deck. Our deck. Jerred was burning burgers.

"God you're right. This is hard."

"There's so many good ones."

"I know, right. What's yours?"

"Gun to my head, it's hard to choose, but gotta be *Top Gun*."

"Okay this is embarrassing, but I haven't seen it."

"What? Are you kidding?"

She shook her head. She wasn't kidding. I tried something. I was holding a bottle of Bud Lime and it became a microphone. (People look at me cockeyed when I order Bud Lime at a restaurant, but they never turn it down at parties. Julia always had a good store of it. Another sign that we were meant to be. Beer-mates.)

"'You never close your eyes anymore when I kiss your lips...'"

"What are you doing?"

I smiled my best Tom Cruise smile, pretended to have confidence.

"'And there's noooooo tenderness like *before* in your fingertips...'"

"Is this from the movie?"

I nodded my head before going down on one knee.

"'You're trying hard not to show it... baby...'"

She smiled. She was loving it. She was grooving.

"Simmer down, Maverick." Fucking Jerred, my Iceman, except if Iceman remained a piece of shit and never had a redemption arc and was holding a tray of desiccated beef.

He put his arm around Julia and said, "Everyone knows the greatest 80s movie is *Animal House*."

"Is that an 80s movie?" she said.

"That's definitely 70s," I said.

"I think I'd know," he said, and that settled it.

He raised his Rolling Rock and said "To Julia's Grand Opening."

"Cheers," I said.

"It really is a grand opening," he said, and pinched her ass and laughed at his joke even as she cringed and sidled away.

. . .

It was, on paper, a bad business idea, yet at the same time it was, and I don't think my devotion to Julia has colored my opinion of her idea, a completely awesome idea, and it became more so as the store came to life.

"There'll be a big John Hughes section here," she said. She had secured the Family Video space, was waiting on someone to come and change it to Timewarp Video. "With posters and maybe like a Molly Ringwald cutout. Right next to the John Candy section. Everyone loves John Candy. Horror over here with Jason and Freddy Krueger cutouts. Always a TV playing an 80s movie. PG-13 or lower of course. Check it out, on the way to the register, you're trapped in a snack maze. Coke. Pepsi. Microwave movie theater butter popcorn. Candy out the ying-yang. This is what you can't get with Netflix, a giant box of Whoppers. It's good right? It's a good idea?"

"Julia," I said, not lying, "it's fucking brilliant."

I guarantee you whatever piece of shit came up with the idea for the plantation-themed steakhouse didn't have to beg the bank to give them the startup money, didn't have to resort to getting the money from some loser guy who wanted to fuck them. That's how this world works. No wonder people are so desperate to pretend, for the length of a dinner, they live in a different one.

"Over here I'm thinking romance. Am I crazy or do they not make romantic movies like they did in the 80s? *Say Anything. Can't Buy Me Love. Dirty Dancing. Romancing the Stone*, I mean, come on, they could never make that movie today. Everyone's so ironic now. Oh and *Pretty Woman*. Oh God do I need a whole Julia Roberts section? Just like a whole shrine to Julia Roberts? My namesake."

"I love it. A shrine to Julia, absolutely. Except Julia Roberts didn't really blow up until the 90s. Yeah," fingering my phone like a nerd, "*Pretty Woman* came out in '90." I held my phone toward her as proof. Fucking nerd.

"Seriously? Well fffff—oh shoot I almost said the f-word."

"Go ahead and say it. I say it all the time."

"I know, but Jerred doesn't like it."

"Pretty sure I've heard him say it more than once. Today."

"I know, but I mean he doesn't like me to say it. It's not ladylike, he says. And my mom always used to say that too."

"Fuck ladylike."

She smiled. It was a real smile, like she was tempted to say it. She thought it was fun.

"Go for it. Say it. Say fuck Julia."

I don't know what I thought would happen. I'd empower her to say "fuck" and she'd melt into my arms and we'd adjourn to the former adults-only section of what used to be Family Video and fuck each other's brains out on the greasy beige carpet that needed to be ripped up and replaced. I didn't think anything would happen. I probably just wanted to beat Jerred at something, useless piece of shit.

"It feels good," I said. "It gives you a release. It's cathartic."

She smiled, but I wasn't going to get her to say it.

"Anyway," I said, "even if *Pretty Woman* came out in 1990 it was still in production in the 80s so in my book that counts."

"You know what, you're right. Thank you. Really, thank you. I haven't said that to you enough."

She gave me a long hug. Our bodies pressed together, the way they were meant to be.

That night I found myself in another empty house, bunk beds in a spare room so the Airbnb owner could squeeze more customers in. The universe meant for us to be together and it was sending me signal after signal. I'd abandoned the robbery scheme, had looked at it from every angle and there was only one way for it to end, with me fucking it all up. Lord knows I needed the money, but I hadn't robbed so much as a penny off the floor. But in the spare room of this empty house there was an antique dresser and on this dresser there was a square black jewelry case with a little ruby necklace inside. It wasn't exactly the *Pretty Woman* necklace, but she'd still love it.

She came in to the shop on my birthday, during the pre-lunch lull when she knew the place would be empty. I wanted to sweep her up but it wasn't my place to make a move, meaning I didn't have the courage.

"I have something for yooooou," she sang, and held up a little box wrapped up all nice.

"I can't believe you remembered."

"Maybe I'm just cyberstalking you," and it was the way she said it that was the gift. The look she gave me. She loved me. She wanted me to love her. I wanted to jump over the counter and take her in my arms but my knees were bad and I was trying to hide my erection.

She set my gift on the counter.

"You didn't have to."

"I know."

I smiled, held her eyes with my eyes. I put everything I felt about her into that look and she smiled in return. There was a look there too.

I reached down to open the gift and she put her hand on top of it but I reached it first so she ended up putting her hand on top of mine. She let it linger for a moment.

"Just remember, it's the thought that counts."

She moved her hand and I unwrapped my present. Inside the box was a tub of Metamucil.

She laughed and said "Happy fortieth old man."

I faked being amused even though I wanted to kill myself.

She tried to justify the gift. "I take it myself," she said. "It makes your poop come out so clean. Like I hardly even need toilet paper. Oh my god, gross. I can't believe I just said that to you. You're so grossed out now."

"No. It's not gross. It's normal. It's natural. It's fine."

"Right? Thanks. Anyway it makes you feel lighter. Like most of this," she mimed having a gut, "it's just poop. This stuff cleans that out and trims you up. It's amazing. It's not just for old people. I was joking about that."

"It's funny," I said. "I love it. Can't wait to try it."

I wanted to cry. I put all my strength into not doing it. It was now safe for me to jump over the counter, if my knees had been up for it anyway.

"And God knows," I said, "after working here all this time I need to trim up. This will be good."

I was hurt but the more I thought about it the more I realized it meant something. It wasn't just anything. It meant she was looking after my well-being. She wanted me to be healthy and regular. And have a clean butthole for whatever she was into. I could be into it too, I figured. And she bought the name-brand. That shit ain't cheap. It had to mean something.

After my shift I went home and got insanely drunk. I kept getting notifications but they weren't people wishing me happy birthday, it was all assembly requests.

I could have made a bundle that night, could have finally got ahead. There had been a big blowout sale at Furniture Mart that weekend and now people were reckoning with the fact that they didn't know how to put anything together, that they'd wasted their lives and were irredeemable. I decided I didn't want to assemble shitty furniture on my birthday. I couldn't figure out how to turn off notifications so I just deleted the whole app. I felt content. Sometimes I will download an app just for the pleasure of deleting it later.

I drank and ate stale donuts while watching a show I don't remember. At some point in the evening the police invited themselves in and put me in handcuffs and smashed a bunch of empties, helped themselves to all my donuts, and kicked a hole in my TV. Some birthday. Fucking sucks getting old.

The fuckers had tracked me down. I can't tell you how many people I know who have been assaulted, raped, robbed, and murdered, and no one was ever brought to justice, no charges ever filed. I get in one brawl with a bunch of racists and suddenly the whole force is a bunch of Sherlock Holmeses.

I avoided jail time the way anyone in this town does, by knowing someone, specifically a judge who wanted to fuck my sister. It's not like she was trading favors for me. These men just wanted to get in good with her. You might be skeptical that a judge, someone who's sworn to uphold the Law, to value it above all else, would compromise himself in this way. All that shows is you don't know any judges. Having a sister who was universally lusted after by members of all sexes was a burden in my teenage and college years because all my friends wanted to fuck her, and in retrospect most of them were only my friends and in at least one case my girlfriend because they wanted to get close to her, but all in all it's been worth it. She used her power to get my sentence converted to six months of house arrest. I had to wear one of those ankle monitors and the cops confiscated my guns. I told them about the Nazi and they told me to go fuck myself. Money down the drain.

I had to explain this to Julia, why I couldn't go to the grand opening. She understood. She was kind of impressed. I think she thought it was kind of hot. I could feel something happening, something building, an electricity.

We were sitting on my deck and I said, "I'm stuck here, but at least I can grill. You want to grill?"

"I could grill."

As always it was the way she said it, this lilt. Killed me.

We got it all set up. Mushrooms and bell peppers and onions and marinated steak cubes. Corn on the cob and pineapple slices. We fired up the grill. We were drinking Bud Limes.

Someone tapped me on the shoulder, the Nissan Nazi. Today he was wearing a red cutoff t-shirt with an

American Flag and the word "FREEDOM" underneath.

He punched me in the throat and when I clutched my throat he punched me in the gut and when I keeled forward he kneed me in the nose and I tumbled backward over the deck rail.

I lay there moaning in the grass and I watched him wheel my grill away out through the gate.

Julia asked if I should call the cops and I said "Fuck the cops."

The Nazi came back and put his boot on my face and said "Keys, bitch. Where are they?"

I told him. He straddled my legs and bent down over my face and said "Next time we take the house. Pay your fucking bills son." On "fucking" he kicked me in the kidney. "I don't care what it takes you're gonna fucking pay us our money."

He left and I had to explain him to Julia. I was barely making enough to make the minimum payments but even then something was always coming up where I had to miss them. I flat out don't know how to make money. It's a sickness. My life is so lonely, and it fills me with sadness and shame, knowing I'll never be a dad, but at least I won't have children who will inherit my debt when I'm gone.

"I don't understand. Why did you give me the money if you didn't really have it?"

"Because," I said, although I didn't know where to take it. Because was it. Because. It should be self-evident.

"Because? Because what though? I mean, I'm grateful. It helped me. I couldn't have done it without your investment. I just don't know why. And I don't want you to be mad at me and think you're gonna lose your house because of me. God how ironic would that be to be in house jail and then lose your house? So why? Why did you give me that check?"

"Because, Julia."

Her eyes knew the answer but they wanted me to say it.

"Because it's you. Because I'd do anything for you. Because your stupidass boyfriend is right. Because I'm in love with you. Because I love you, Julia."

She smiled. We were sitting on the steps of the deck, side by side. She twisted and put her hand on my elbow and said, "Can I give you a kiss?"

I laughed. I was dying. I said yes. I said, "Yes, Julia, you can give me a kiss."

And she did. One kiss. One very moderate smooch on the lips and she turned and left. I was dead. I followed her inside, all sad-puppy-like, and from the window watched her walk out to her car and get in and drive away. Julia.

The night before the grand opening Julia texted me kind of late. "Big day tomorrow!!!"

I smiled, I watched the three dots in the text bubble as she kept typing. A new message popped up: "Wish u could be there."

A longer bubbly ellipsis followed, one that was full of possibilities, full of hope. Finally the text appeared and it made me so happy. It said "I broke up with Jerred…"

I typed and deleted a hundred replies, but I didn't send any of them. I didn't know what to say. I didn't want to come on too strong or seem too eager. I didn't know what to say so I didn't say anything. Classic aloof approach. I couldn't sleep after that.

When I was a kid I would lie awake at night thinking about the end of the world. How the sun will die one day. How every human will be long dead before then. In this regard I have always stayed young at heart. I got to thinking about death. About being dead and how the world will go on without me and I'll be locked in a coffin or, worse, I'll be ashes in an urn that no one knows what to do with. I get shaky when I think like this, terrified, crazy. Death is total bullshit. When I die I don't want to be buried. I want to be brought back no matter what the consequences. Shock me. Download me. Turn me into a vegetable I don't give a fuck. Every stupid little thing we do, everything that's wrong with us individually and societally, is because we know we're going to die one day. We know too much. We shouldn't know the sun is going to die one day and that the Earth will be dead before that even happens and that humans will have been extinct for a long-ass time before that even happens. We spend our life savings on horse semen, we wash our cars in the blood of the lamb, we eat at theme restaurants and hand over $20,000 checks to an old flame in a desperate attempt to be loved, because this knowledge has broken our brains.

I couldn't bear it. I was as insane as everyone else. Insane with love. An insane person surrounded by insane people. What is it with this place? The thought of living without her, of dying without her, was unbearable. My brain was about to explode. I decided to text her back, to not leave her hanging because life is too short for aloofness, if I had even a slim chance with Julia I didn't want to let another second go by where I wasn't going for it with my whole being, but by then it was three a.m., too late or early to text, and when I set my phone on the nightstand I bumped the black necklace case and I got a better idea.

. . .

I was going to that fucking opening. All I needed was to google how to unlock an ankle monitor. Lot of cops in the forums telling you not to even try, seriously if you're lucky enough to be on house arrest instead of in jail don't even tempt fate, GPS anti-tamper technology yada-fucking-yada but all I needed was some Reynolds wrap and a little tape.

I'd had my coffee and taken my multivitamin and drunk my protein shake (cum-free) and my fiber (she was so right about the fiber, of course she was right). I was ready for my day. I was ready for Julia. Was she ready for me? All I needed was some wheels.

My neighbor Pete The Meat, who had sold me that Dodge Neon, was out in his yard grilling breakfast. All-beef sausage and turkey bacon. Known as Pete The Meat since grade school, he had grown into his name, turning into one of these all-meat-diet freaks, type of guy that believes he'll survive the apocalypse by hunting deer and small game but will end up turning into a zombie from eating deer infected with chronic wasting disease. Sort of the anti-Hank Hill, Pete The Meat believed grilling with charcoal was the only effective way to cook meat. He made good money as a dealer. Cars and drugs. Sometimes both. A fully synergized business. (Which why the fuck didn't I just start dealing? All that time I could have been robbing pills from people's houses.) He had a truly enviable grill setup, with a double-barrel smoker, a portable grill, and a Big Green Egg, as well as a fire pit. His big dream was to open up a theme restaurant called Grillroy Was Here that would only serve meat cooked over coals and would only play music by his favorite band, Styx.

"Mornin', Pete," I said all cheery. I had never felt better. I was gliding, hovering above the earth like a madly-in-love ghost whose dreams were this close to coming true.

"Mornin' bruh. Not to be rude, but it's Pete The Meat. Not just Pete."

"Oh. Yeah, sorry, Pete. The Meat."

"Yeah it's all good. Names are important is all. I ain't mad. It's just about respect."

"For sure, man."

"You okay bruh? You usually remember that."

"I am. I am. I'm just like super preoccupied at the moment. Honestly I have sort of a weird favor to ask. The Neon got, I don't know, confiscated I guess you'd call it, and I really need to borrow your car."

"My ride?" Holding up a paper plate bending under the weight of an unsanitary amount of sausage and turkey bacon, "You want some breakfast bruh?"

I waved away the breakfast and said, "I hate to even ask, but…"

"Let me stop you there. I can see it in your eyes bruh. Just answer me this: Do you need my ride for love?"

"Man I wouldn't even ask if it was anything else."

He set the plate down and went back to grill work.

"Bruh it's 100% copacetic. I'm a romantic through and through. Plus I've seen your girl and she's as smoking as this grill. My ride is your ride. But bruh let me give you some advice, you got to get on this all-meat thing. It ain't a fad, it's simply mother nature. Look at me."

He was shirtless and in fairness pretty shredded. He tightened his abs. His abs had abs.

"Only thing I'm gonna say is you won't catch me desperate to borrow another man's ride to go chasing some chickie cuz the chickies chase me. You feel me? It's the meat. The meat. I'm serious, man, it's good for your health and it makes you fuck like a wild mustang and women can sense it. Changes your pheromones. Only three things I eat and that's meat, pussy, and ass, in that order. Little tip, you want to really get a lady interested you don't got to give her jewelry, just give her Metamucil. Don't cheap out with the generic shit either, get that name-brand shit. Lets her know you eat ass. She'll appreciate it. She'll appreciate the hell out of it if you get my drift."

Awoooga, Julia, what are you into?!

"And also get some for yourself because even if your girl won't eat ass on the all-meat diet you will need a little help in the poop department. Bruh get some of this sausage. Take it, nah take it."

I ate the meat. I wasn't hungry, I was too amped up to eat, but for the privilege of borrowing my neighbor's black 2016 Dodge Charger so I could go win my girl I was happy to eat it. Pete The Meat was fucking ecstatic to give me the keys.

This was my grand gesture, the 80s movie climax where it looks like the guy has fucked it all up but he goes all in on some over-the-top romantic gesture. My John Cusack in *Say Anything* moment. I tuned the radio to 103.9 *80s 80s and More 80s* and I shit you not God himself had queued up the theme from *Top Gun*, Kenny Loggins' greatest song, "Danger Zone." Something was finally going my way. I peeled out.

...

There's a logic to roundabouts, but it was the devil that brought them to Missouri. I normally would have taken a different route, but I didn't have time. I had to make haste. I took my life in my hands, pulling into the roundabout like a surfer dropping into a wave. A red Kia flew into my lane and I swerved into the turn lane, now cut off from the exit I needed. Not a big deal. I kept my cool. I circled around and asserted my position. I was all set to come around and hit my exit. I had the right of the way. A lady in a white Toyota Sienna really wanted to jump her turn but I stared her down and she froze. A gray Nissan Cube materialized in my rearview. Bogey on my tail. I thought maybe it was a coincidence but the way he rode my ass let me know he was on to me. I missed the exit again and stayed in the circle. He moved to pull around me, thinking he was going to cut me off, him and his little Cube. I said fuck it and I floored it. I was in a fucking Charger after all. Screamed around the roundabout like a missile, swerved around a CRV and flew in between a

Prius and a new-model Malibu. The Nazi slammed into the rear of the Malibu and I was clear.

The place was packed, made me really happy. Julia, in a *Pretty in Pink* prom dress, was surprised to see me. I was surprised to see Jerred. Like me he hadn't thought to dress to fit the theme, although I had a better reason. I could have kicked his ass.

I gave her a look and she shrugged and said, "You didn't text back."

"I've got something for you."

I should have practiced. I should have made sure it was second nature. I held open the jewelry box and the necklace flashed at her.

"For me?"

I nodded. She reached for the necklace and I slammed the lid on her fingers. I don't know what made me think I could be as smooth as Richard Gere. Like what in my whole life had led me to believe I would ever be able to pull that off?

"Ow," she said. "Why'd you do that?"

"I'm sorry, I didn't mean to, it was from the movie. But here, take it. It's for you, for your grand opening."

"How did you…?"

"Just take it."

She did. She had to go. She had people to see. Movies to rent out. Whoppers to sell. Felt like the whole town was there, crammed into this one video store. A guy from the paper, news crews from all three TV stations.

"Can we talk?"

I saw Deb and Chuck in the horror section, next to Freddy and Jason, and avoided eye contact. There was Cara, holding up DVDs of *Back to School* and *Back to the Future*, looking like this was too big a decision for her to make by herself, but she had no one to help her make it. In another life, with a friendlier Fate, who knows, it could have been me. My sister grabbed my arm and wanted to know what the fuck I was doing there.

"Relax, sis." I pointed to the foil-wrapped ankle monitor.

"What the fuck is wrong with you?"

"I couldn't not be here. I'm sorry but I can't talk right now. I have to talk to Julia."

"Dude," she said, but I didn't hear anything else. The whole world just quit existing for me. Like I knew they were there, I could see horse guy with a box full of horse cum pleading with Julia to let him have some space in the snack maze but he wasn't real to me. "I'm begging you," I heard him say, this man who wasn't even real, "there's a crisis in masculinity."

"Julia."

Then the anti-siren activist was trying to foist some literature on her, a sign for the window, little fact sheets to set by the register, a handmade zine.

"Julia."

My arms stretched out to reach her. Something held me back. Roger tried to talk to me, something about my sister. He was clinging to me so I grabbed a DVD off the shelf. *Toxic Avenger 2.* It held precisely no meaning but he held it like it meant everything.

"Julia."

She was on the other side of the store now. There was no path to her. I could hear her say my name though. I could see her looking for me. I cried out her name. I looked all around me. The people were real again and they all stared at me, an impenetrable wall of flesh. There was no choice but to *Crocodile Dundee 2* it. I climbed up on a display table, knocking over a squadron of *Policy Academy* DVDs. A metal water pipe ran the length of the room and I held onto it to stay steady. I said "You" to a beefy nerd in a *Ghostbusters* t-shirt. We made eye contact. Without words he understood my plan and made himself available. I stepped out. I put myself in his hands, or on his shoulder, so to speak. A leap of faith. It worked. Others saw the display and a path cleared up, a path of sturdy shoulders. Soon I came to the horse guy, wild-eyed and frantic, but strong. He nodded his assent and I stepped across the void. When my weight was upon him he buckled like a lame horse. All that testosterone had turned his heart to mush. I held onto the pipe until it burst. I crashed to the ground, breaking my ankle and its electronic monitor. Water rained down on us with violence and fury. Through my agony I heard Julia crying. She forced her way through the crowd, and I could only think if only she'd done that before. Soaked to her core, her dress clinging to her the way I longed to be clinging to her, she looked even more beautiful. My Julia. She screamed at me "What the fuck is wrong with you?" and melted into her stupidass boyfriend's arms. I'd finally got her to say it.

Walnuts

Juanita lost a whole year of her life. Her sister wrapped the birth certificate in an oversized box, weighted with her ex's golf balls. Patty tied it up in ribbon and made a pretty bow. She thought it would be funny. "I found it in one of dad's old boxes," she said at the party, which consisted of herself and Juanita and Juanita's son James. There was fried chicken and potato salad. The cake was sugar-free because of Juanita's diabetes. "I thought you'd get a kick out of it. I thought you'd want to know." Juanita was turning seventy, only now it was seventy-one, the first year of what could be her last decade on Earth just vanished like a popped bubble. All she could think to say was "I wish I didn't know this."

Later that same year she also lost her baby. He was fifty-four at the time but still her baby. They're always your baby. He was up in Iowa. She almost never got to see him. At the funeral she realized it was the first time she'd seen Joe's boys since they were little. She'd lost those years too.

Back home, James tried to comfort her. He said "Momma, I'm sorry I couldn't be as good a boy as Joe was but I'm gonna do better. I'm gonna be a better man. I'm gonna be more like my big brother. It's never too late to change, Momma." All she could think to say was "It hurts so much I wish he'd never been born."

That killed him. That cemented it. He'd made the promise before but he was bound to stick to it after that. The life he led, he should have been the one that died first. He was on his way to dying, the drinking, the other stuff. But he was done.

James had done pretty much every job in Oklahoma his record would allow. He'd framed houses and worked in the oil fields, he'd held the stop/go sign on paving projects, a hundred degrees out in the boondocks, he'd washed dishes and stocked shelves and mowed lawns. He couldn't afford his own riding mower but working on a landscaping crew had given him the idea to start his own business cleaning dog poop in people's yards. He had even come up with a funny name for the company, Poo Patrol, after the cartoon his grandkids were obsessed with, but there just weren't enough customers. Nothing ever stuck. At the moment he was between jobs. He was looking for opportunities but they were like four-leaf clovers. Joe could come upon a patch of clover, look down, and then he'd say "Well would you look at that, I can't believe I found one." James had never found one.

After Joe and her birthday, Juanita was convinced this was another year of loss. Trouble always comes in threes. The last time this happened her daughters had moved to Texas and a twister took her house and cancer took her husband. And there was the year she lost the baby in May and she lost her mother in June and her father in July. He hadn't even been sick, it was her ma who'd been sick. She didn't want to know what the third loss would be this year. She hoped it was simply herself.

James thought with Joe gone his mother would be too much. She'd always be calling him, she'd always be needing something, she'd be always in his business, but it was the opposite. She could care less.

He came around more. He had always come around a lot but it was always when he needed something, money, dinner, cigarettes. He started to do little things for her, nice things. He'd borrow the neighbor's mower and cut the grass. He'd get out early in the morning and weed the garden. He'd go pick up her groceries. She didn't even notice. Up to now he had always been a taker, in his relationship with his mother. He was always eating her food. He'd walk the two blocks from his trailer and burst in unannounced through the back door and stand in the middle of the kitchen eating whatever was handy. Juanita always marveled at his constant standing. He had never liked to sit. "I got too much energy, Momma. Too much to do, too much to see to stand here sitting." He made one of his famous back-door entrances that summer and made himself a tomato sandwich, a whole tomato from the garden, sliced thick and with a heavy sprinkling of salt and pepper, between two pieces of skillet toast. Juanita couldn't fathom how he stayed so thin. He still ate like a seventeen-year-old trying to make the football team.

"Momma," he said through the sandwich, "something I gotta tell you. It's been weighing on me all these years. Them pecan trees, the ones in the back yard, I told you the ice storm got them that Christmas you went to Texas to see the girls, but Momma there was no ice storm. Not bad enough to take out them two pecan trees. A guy just come to the door one day when I was here making a sandwich and he offered to buy them. And I needed money. It was when I was still using. I'm sorry, Momma. I know how much you loved them pecan trees."

"They were walnuts, Jimmy. Not pecans. I really wished you hadn't told me."

James woke up the next day with an idea. He hadn't felt better at all when he told her. If anything he felt worse, seeing as he hadn't thought about the trees in years. He had wanted the truth to make him feel better, to make her feel better, but it hit him that an apology was not the same thing as atonement. You have to make good. You cut down a tree you plant a new one. He decided to drive down to Owasso.

He knew the girl at the nursery, although she wasn't a girl. She was a full-grown woman, just like he was a full-grown man, but it had never felt that way. He had kids and grandkids but he only ever felt old when he looked in the mirror. She was a few years younger than him. She looked good. She was always pretty but some girls, some women, lose their prettiness at a certain age, but Alice was prettier than ever. She smiled when she saw him. She put her hand on his shoulder, just briefly, softly. She casually mentioned that she was recently divorced. She didn't have to tell him that, she just happened to work it into a conversation about walnut trees. He didn't ask for her number. He thought he'd surprise her. His buddy Jeff was seeing one of her friends and he knew he could get it that way. It would impress her, show her he was really interested and he was the kind of guy to take initiative. Maybe that would make up for also being the kind of guy who didn't have a job or any opportunities. He did some math in his head and figured he could afford to take her to Outback and splurge on drinks and dessert if she wanted it. The tree cost way more than he'd planned but what else was money for? Still, he'd decided to only buy one tree even though it should have been two. It was the gesture anyway, that was what mattered more than the number of trees or how much they cost. The Stones came on the radio, "Angie," his favorite song, and he turned it up and drove faster. He wanted to get home.

When he came up to the first stoplight in town he called and said "Hey Momma, I want you to walk out in the back yard. I got a surprise for you." She was waiting for him when he pulled up, that look on her face like she was a pod person. That look broke his heart. That look told him that nothing he could do for her would matter now, that he didn't even matter now. If he died, if he was the third thing, it wouldn't break her heart at all. He smiled big but it was a lie. He no longer felt happy about what he'd done. He didn't know how he felt. But he kept up the act. He rolled down his window and pointed back behind him and said "Well would you look at that!" She walked up to the bed of the truck and said "You brought me a stick in a plastic pot. I guess you could call this a surprise."

He scrambled out of the cab of his dead stepdad's old Ford, saying "No, no no no no." He found himself staring at the keypad on his phone, like this was some sort of tree emergency and there was a tree 911 he was supposed to call. "What kind of place sells you trees that the leaves fall off before you even get them home?"

"You didn't think to lay it down, Jimmy?"

"Nobody told me to lay it down, Momma. Why didn't she tell me to lay it down?"

Juanita didn't answer. When he was loading it James had placed the tree's pot inside the well of an old tire and bungied the trunk to hold it steady. He had thought he was being clever. He thought that would protect it. He could have died right there, but you can't think that way, you can't give up, you have to think positive, when the wind strips away your leaves you can still grow new ones.

"They'll grow back, Momma. You and me, we're gonna plant this tree. Just you wait. It don't look like much right now but one day it'll be a beautiful tree."

All Juanita could think to say was "Who'll even be left to see it?"

The Sun Still Shines on a Dog's Ass

All I wanted was to go fishing. I couldn't take my truck because my wife had took it in the divorce and between rent and beer and alimony I could never save up enough to buy a new one. And there was a little issue with my license. I got around most places on foot, which had the pleasing effect of cutting twenty pounds around my waist, but my favorite spot was too far to walk and it was hot as sin already. I thought about calling my mom but I knew she'd give me hell for wasting the day at the strip pits instead of looking for a job and I didn't have the energy to think up a convincing lie, not in that heat.

I had two neighbors, neither one of whom I wanted to spend the day fishing with. People called us The Three Yahoos. We were these sad bachelors living out in nowheresville, the edge of town where you can't tell if it's still town or the sticks. If you could call what we did living. I didn't mind that people said that about us even if it wasn't very clever.

Rick was my neighbor about half a mile to the north. He had this nice little Toyota pickup with four doors and good air conditioning, but you didn't want to knock on his door unannounced. He was one of these anti-government people whose yard was littered with homemade landmines and if you managed to sneak your way through his front yard without getting blasted to smithereens he still might just pop out from behind a tree and shoot you. He didn't have a cell phone, you just had to hail him on the CB radio and I didn't see the point. It was just too hot for any type of nonsense.

I walked down to Dale's house. All he had was this old truck from the eighties. A Chevy. It didn't have AC but it did have those nifty truck windows that open from the side to give you a good cross breeze. And it had that little sliding window in the back that I always liked because you can set a cooler there in the truck bed and reach through the window when you want a beer. People talk about horsepower and torque, but what really makes a truck is a cooler full of cold beer. The problem with Dale was he was a vegetarian, and he would want to bring his dog along. Took that mutt almost everywhere he went. Dale loved that dog. Relative to getting shot in the face by a paranoid maniac with a trust fund, a little fishing trip with hippie Dale didn't sound that bad.

I call him a hippie but he probably wasn't one in the traditional sense. He was just kind of an odd duck. Not that I'm one to talk.

Dale smiled and waved when he saw me walking up his gravel drive and he said he wouldn't mind at all giving me a lift out to the pits. It occurs to me that "strip pits" sounds a little unseemly but all it means is when they were mining coal around southeast Kansas back in the day they used these big machines to dig up the surface material and the holes that got left behind eventually filled up with water and now the Department of Wildlife keeps them stocked with rainbow trout and channel catfish.

"Let me grab my gear," Dale said, "and holler for old Duke and we'll head out."

Dale had a real nice garden with big red juicy tomatoes and strawberries and sweet corn and all kinds of good stuff. It was a garden to be proud of and just looking at those tomatoes I was hoping he'd offer me just one, I'd sit there and eat that thing just like an apple, but he didn't say anything and I was too polite to ask. He grabbed an old coffee can off his little potting bench and filled it with worms out of the compost heap.

"Nice garden," I said.

"Thank you."

"Real nice."

"Yep. Been a good season. Lot a rain. Not too much rain."

And that was that.

We walked back to the truck. He settled his rod and tackle box in the truck bed and went in the house while I piddled around outside. I wasn't sure how long he'd be inside and I couldn't decide if it would be worth it to let the tailgate down so as to have a place to sit, or if that would be presumptuous, but before long he come out of the house with a blue cooler, and that made me feel better about choosing Dale to ask to be my fishing buddy for the day.

"Grabbed us some ice cold beer," he told me, "and a couple fresh tomatoes." He pronounced "tomatoes" the way God intended, "tomatuhs." "You like tomatoes?"

"Do I like tomatoes? Shit I'd eat a homegrown tomato just like it was an apple."

That made him smile. He liked that and I began to feel like this was going to be a real nice fishing trip.

He set the cooler in the back of the truck and told me to grab a beer if I wanted one. I got a cold beer out of the cooler and by the time I got the can open it was hot but it still tasted good. I said we'd need to run by my place and grab my rod and he just nodded and opened the passenger door and said "Go on, Duke. Up you go buddy."

I said, "You let that dog ride up front with you?"

"Sure. Old Duke goes just about everywhere with me."

"Most people make their dogs ride in the back."

"Most people ain't quite civilized," he said, and it wasn't like I could disagree with that statement.

I hesitated, and he said "He don't bite," and I climbed in and Dale shut the door for me, real ginger-like like we were on a date.

After we picked up my gear Dale insisted that we stop at the McDonald's in town before we went on out to the pits. "Duke loves McDonald's," he said.

I never saw nothing like it. Dale, a grown man, ordered a Coke, a Big Mac, and a vanilla cone. We sat in that truck, two yahoos and a mongrel, and I ate myself some French fries and a burger and watched in horror as he traded licks of that vanilla cone with his old dog. When they were done with the ice cream Dale unwrapped the Big Mac, slid the beef patty out and fed it to his dog, and then Dale ate the bun with ketchup, pickle, lettuce, and tomato. Some vegetarian, I thought, but I didn't say anything.

You might be wondering, how in the world is it lunchtime already and they haven't even got out to the fishing spot? Well, there are people who believe in timing their fishing trips just right. There are people who keep track of what time of day the fish bite best at all the different fishing spots in their locality. There are whole websites dedicated to catering to the fastidious whims of these people, snobs in my opinion. I am not one of these people. And in my defense it was only around eleven, still technically morning. Besides, one of the pleasures of fishing is sitting around complaining about not getting any bites, which you can do any time of day.

Well I was sitting there in the cab of Dale's old Silverado, just minding my own business, munching away on my burger and trying to ignore the disturbing display of a fifty-year-old man devouring a pattiless burger, when I saw her. I flat couldn't believe it. And to make matters worse, she saw me. You've heard the expression "The dog that bit the car." I don't mean to imply anything negative about my wife, it is after all just an expression, but there are some dogs that when they bite the car they know precisely what to do with it, and it is in that sense that I say my ex-wife Bev, whom I hadn't laid eyes on in near two years, looked like the dog that bit the car.

"Quick," I said with a mouthful of burger, "get this son of a bitch started," but it was too late. The woman was quick on her feet and we were slow on ours.

Dale spilled his Coke and Duke sneaked the last bit of my burger in the shuffle to bug out but all our trouble was pointless, which I take now to be a metaphor. Bev sidled right up to the truck and inserted herself right inside through my open window. I didn't know what to expect, aside from the worst, and my heart seized up and I thought I was going to die right there with my ex-wife's head looming over me.

"Carl, you big dumbass," she said, "I need your help!"

Well I knew better than to get involved, but I couldn't help it either. It was fate. Or predestination. Something. Whatever your belief system there was no not doing it. Our souls were welded together, two rusted-out pieces of metal not even worth scrapping, joined up for eternity. Me and Bev had already been married and divorced three times and I was afraid what would happen. I might could survive a tornado or a shootout with the police but I couldn't survive another heartbreak. Fool me once, shame on you. Fool me four times, shit, I don't even know. Skeptics will say it's cliché to attribute my multiple DWIs to my woman troubles, but it is objective, scientific fact that the reason I was in Dale's truck instead of already out on the pits with a line in the water and a cold beer in my hand was because that woman had broke my heart, then put it back together, then broke it again and repaired it again only to break it again even worse than the first two times. The last time we got together the way it happened was she knocked on my door one night and she said "My septic's backed up on me and I don't have the money to get it pumped and I really gotta poop" and there was just something in the way she said she had to poop, I can't describe it, but the next thing you know she was practically moved in. This time it's bound to work, we said. Third time's a charm, we said. Let me tell you, the third time is a whamdoozie. The third time breaks your spirit, like a wild horse that's just been so abused it dies on the inside and lives the rest of its life as an in-the-flesh ghost. The third time's a curse. The fourth time, I couldn't even imagine what hell lay in store for me. I was both the character in a horror movie, too stupid and clueless to turn around and walk away, get free of danger, and the audience screaming "TURN AROUND YOU BIG DUMBASS, DON'T GO THROUGH THAT DOOR." Naturally I went through the door, as if I was an actor just following a really bad script. I might have had my doubts but it was right there in the script.

She laid it all out. She'd fell behind on some bills and decided the only way to make it up was to try her luck at the casino, and when that didn't work she borrowed money from some dudes, the type of dudes you definitely don't want to owe money to, and now she was late paying them back and the only way she could see to get the money was to rob a bank.

"I wasn't feeling optimistic, let me tell you, but then you boys come along at just this moment. That can only be a sign from God."

"More out of curiosity than anything," said Dale, "but what bank are you trying to rob?"

"Arvest Bank down on Third."

"All that alimony," I said, "and it still ain't enough to cover your gambling debts."

"You hush, old man. You don't know my affairs. If you gotta know I was laid up in the hospital with appendicitis and that shit's expensive. I swear to God, you save your money and don't buy them new shoes you want even though they're on sale just so you can stay on top of everything and all of a sudden a completely useless part of your body breaks down and you're gonna die if you don't have an expensive surgery and the next thing you know you're in debt up past your tits to the Irish mafia. But I believe this'll work. I swear my big problem was I had concocted the perfect three-man plan and all I been needing was the other two men and here you are."

"Yep," I said. "Here we are."

"Well. Are you in or what?"

She wasn't asking Dale. He didn't even factor. It was just natural that he'd be in. If there was one thing Dale hated more than hamburgers it was Arvest Bank. This man had once spent a week standing outside of an Arvest Bank, holding a sign that said "Arvest Bank Stole My Money." Until the dang cops hauled him away. It'd been something about overdrafts.

There was no fighting fortune. I may be a dumbass but I ain't a fool.

I'm in," I said. "I'm in, I'm in."

"Good. Scoot over."

So we headed for the bank.

"Well, said Bev, "we really are packed in here."

I was in the middle with the dog on my lap, his hot breath in my face, the warmth of Bev's leg against mine.

"Here's the plan," she said. "Dale I guess you're the getaway driver seeing how this is your truck and Mr. DWI over here no longer has a license."

"I don't see how that's pertinent," I said, but she was off on her plan and she didn't hear me.

Bev would go in first, posing as a customer. Exactly five minutes later I was supposed to go in with a ski mask she handed me over my face. She gave me a handgun to wave around, as well, but it wasn't real.

"Now what in hell am I supposed to do with this?"

"It's just theater, Carl. No one's going to inspect it, we just need it to put the fear of God in people."

"Well what if there's some hotshot in there with a real gun who decides he wants to be a hero? I ain't getting shot today, Bev. Not today."

"Well that's why you'll have me as your hostage. You run straight to me and grab me from behind and point that gun at my head and scream 'EVERYONE ON THE FLOOR' and then you're gonna look at the Brinks man and say 'Not you.' Got it? We're not even gonna mess with the tellers or the vault, all we want is that Brinks man. This bank is real sloppy, they just take it in right through the front door and I've got their schedule worked out."

Dale piped in then. He said, "Question. Won't this aforesaid Brinks man be armed?"

"He will be armed," said Bev, "but here's the thing: he happens to be in love with me and he won't let this dumbass," meaning me, which I'm sure was clear anyway, "shoot me. He'll probably be slow on his feet anyway because I put a little Benadryl and laxative in his coffee this morning."

"Now Bev . . ."

I hated that Brinks man as a rival, but I also felt a sense of solidarity with him. We were rivals, but we were brothers. Of course I would have put the laxative in his coffee myself if she'd asked me to.

"Don't you Now Bev me you son of a bitch."

The truck jerked to a stop and old Duke flung back against the stereo and I was flat stunned to see we were at the bank. Up until now it had all been theoretical, but here we were at the scene of the crime, preparatory to the crime.

Bev got out and shut the door and leaned back in through the window and said "Five minutes. Not four. Five. Synchronize your watch."

"That ain't how that works," I said, but she was gone. God, that woman. I watched her walk and I could feel those feelings.

"This is a bad idea," I said, and Dale said "I don't know, seems like she's got it all worked out" and I didn't say nothing.

The robbery went okay. It was almost unremarkable, kind of anticlimactic for the most part. Pretty good for our first robbery, I'd say. All according to plan.

The only hiccup was as we were heading out the door this woman was coming in and she looked at us but apparently didn't see my fake gun or the heavy-duty briefcases we were holding. She goes "Well hey girl" and Bev just snapped at her, she said "SHUT UP, CAROL!"

Dale pulled up and we threw the money in the back of his truck and split. Somehow I got stuck in the middle seat again with the dog on me.

"You know," said Dale after a few minutes of no one saying anything, "it does occur to me that I shouldn't have used my truck for the getaway vehicle. And that I should have also been wearing a mask."

"Well I only had the one mask," said Bev.

"Nevertheless," said Dale.

"Let's just get to the spot. I'm not worried about it," said Bev, but you could tell she was worried about it, that she'd realized there was a small little hole in her plan. It was like the time during our second marriage when we lived there on Twentieth and I rented a little excavator this one time because Bev got it in her head that we needed a koi pond. "It'll be peaceful," she told me. "We'll set out by the koi pond and meditate. You're gonna love it babe." It was a nice idea but the problem was I accidentally hit the water line. It wasn't that hard to fix, I just went to the hardware store and got some one-inch PVC and a couple of couplers and some pipe cleaner and cement glue. I had a lot of trouble cutting my pipe to the right length and getting it to line up right with this tee in the line, so I dry fit everything to make sure I knew the exact size to cut my pipe. Well that worked but I noticed once I turned the water back on there was a little leak where I had forgot to glue the end of the pipe where it goes in to the coupler.

I tried to help by saying "Maybe your friends can get us a car. Maybe they can get rid of this one."

"Yeah but that shit costs money," she said. "Everything costs money, Carl."

It didn't take long to get to the drop point, which was a gravel yard south of town. I had to chuckle as we pulled in and I saw one of them thin blue line flags flying on the gate. That was pretty smart. That was pretty funny.

"Hey Bev," I called after her.

"What hon?"

"Something I've always wondered."

"What's that?"

"Well," I don't know why I thought this was going to be funny. "Ask your friends if they know where old Jimmy Hoffa's buried."

She smiled.

"You always were a character."

I liked it when she said that. There's not anything else remarkable about me. It made me feel good and I should've known better.

"Some people get so caught up being a character they forget how to just be a person."

"Now I don't know what that means, Bev."

"Think on that," she said. "You think on that."

Like hell.

Bev went up to this guy and I heard him say "Five minutes." Everything was five minutes. I can't speak for the others but I was getting antsy. I filled the time by making chitchat.

"I got a question for you Dale."

"Shoot."

"Well I thought you was a vegetarian but here you are heading out to go fishing with me."

"Well I don't eat meat but I'll eat me some fish now and then."

"Ah."

Old Duke, who had slid over into Bev's seat like water finding level, well he sighed and laid his head on my leg.

A couple minutes went by and the guy who'd told Bev five minutes got a phone call and when he got off he said "He says he's held up and to just give me the money."

He was a jacked-up white guy with a goatee and wraparounds. He was counting a fat wad of cash just as nonchalant as nonchalant could be. I could scrap in my day but he would have kicked my ass, I ain't too proud to admit it.

Bev made to hand over the briefcases but then she stopped and I heard her say "This ain't right" and my throat closed up tight.

"What's not right, lady?"

"This is mine," she said. "I worked for this. I risked my dang life for this money. I devised the perfect plan for this money. Them boys in that truck risked their lives for this money. They deserve their share."

He sort of perked up and Bev said "Nope. Uh-uh. No deal."

The dude's eyes went wide and he goes "Just give me the money, bitch" and I said "Dale, run this son of a bitch over." You could tell the dude heard Dale put the truck in gear but it didn't quite register and by the time he thought to run he was already flying forward. He landed in a tangle and Bev run up to the truck and tossed the money back in the bed. Then she stopped.

"Bev, what're you doing? What are you doing Bev?"

She ran over and picked up that fat wad of cash he'd been holding. She run back to the truck and opened the door but Dale started driving before she was in, and I reached over the dog and grabbed her arm and she rode on the running board.

"Dale what the—" Well I saw what the, it was a gun. The dude was pointing a gun at us. Not for long though because Dale drove right over his leg. It sounds awful when I say it like that, but shit you should have heard the sound of this dude's leg getting run over by a truck, if you want to talk about awful. You might not sleep for a while. He hit the dude's leg twice, once with the front passenger tire and once with the rear. We were all quiet. Bev scooted the dog over and got herself settled and Dale made our second big getaway of the day.

Duke was sitting squeezed in between me and Bev and he had his sad old bird dog head resting on top of the truck seat, just staring out the back window.

We all stayed pretty cool. For three people who were wanted by the fuzz and whatever kind of hooligans Bev had got mixed up with we were pretty damn sanguine. Or we seemed that way. You never know what's going on inside someone's head, or at least I don't.

Dale said, "Where to?" and Bev said "Mexico. Let's go to Mexico. We'll go to Mexico. We'll drink margaritas."

Mexico, I thought. Shit, I thought. I remember thinking I could go for one of them fish tacos, but I don't think I said anything about it. I was processing the day's events. I didn't have anything useful to say at that juncture so I just kept quiet for a while. I had things to ponder and I could feel them closing in on us, the way a dog that's scared of storms will start to shaking long before you hear the thunder.

It was kind of a bummer not having a driver's license or a car but the way I got to looking at it was my old Husqvarna got me where I needed to go and there wasn't any law, as far as I could tell, about drinking and driving on a riding mower. Plus I didn't have to pay car insurance. Once it became a lifestyle choice instead of a punishment I couldn't see myself ever going back to the old way of being tied down to an automobile. Other than that it was a pain in the rear to get out to the strip pits. I was starting to freak out a little bit, just sitting there thinking about our situation, all the things that could go wrong. I was thinking how funny a thing life is, I had gone to Dale's looking for a ride because I didn't want to get shot knocking on Rick's door, and now I couldn't picture any scenario that didn't end with my body filled with bullet holes.

It didn't take long before we noticed someone on our tail. Dale thought maybe it was just an asshole driver but Bev looked in the rearview and said it was them. Then she went back to fiddling with her phone. She had downloaded an app that lets you listen to the police scanner, which was handy but also nerve-wracking.

The car behind us veered left and sped up to overtake us and Dale said "Are you sure?" and Bev said "Uh huh" and Dale swerved and caught their front end with his tail and ran their asses right off the road.

"Jesus, Dale."

"No backseat driving," he said.

I will say that son of a bitch was the epitome of grace under pressure. Just as cool as could be.

Bev shut off her cell phone and tossed it out the window.

"Boys," she said. "I got bad news. It seems likely that we're all gonna die. The pigs is on our trail and it's just a matter of time till they catch up to us."

We were approaching the Neosho River. I wished we could just pull off and go fishing.

"I'm sorry, boys. I really thought we could pull this off."

We passed a truck broke down on the side of the road. It was not the sort of truck you would expect to see broke down on the side of the road. It wasn't brand new but you could tell it was well cared for. It was a green Ford F-150 with a long bed and a green topper. I took it as a sign from the heavens and I said "Stop the truck, Dale." He slowed but didn't stop and I said "Damn it, Dale, you stop this damn truck this damn instant. Back up, back up to that truck."

"What the hell," said Bev. "Even if you knew how to hotwire a car there ain't no use hot-wiring a car that's busted down on the side of the road."

She's right about me being a big dumbass. You and I may achieve the same results, but I will have done so by the most convoluted means possible, and that's what makes me a surpassing dumbass. Sometimes that's just what you need.

"Y'all won't believe this but I got an idea."

Dale had pulled back so he was right in front of the green Ford, and I told him to get out and help me, and I crawled out his side behind him.

I don't know if my guardian angel worked out a deal with the guardian angel of whoever owned that truck or what, but it was lucky that topper wasn't locked. Otherwise my plan wouldn't have worked. But

I popped that window open and put down the tailgate and me and Dale went to work detaching the topper. Bev was yelling at me but she didn't get out of the truck. We didn't have time to argue, we just had to act. I was sorry to steal someone's topper like that but it had to be done.

Soon enough Bev did get out though and she come over and said "With all the money you got now you could just buy you a truck topper, instead of stealing one. We gotta get outta here first though."

"This ain't a truck topper, Bev. It's a boat."

"Like hell," said Dale, but he still helped me load it in his truck because I had seized the moment. We were married to the plan now.

"Let me drive," I said.

"But you don't got a license," said Bev, and then she laughed.

Half a mile down the road there was a pulloff that went down to the river. It was back in the woods on someone's property. I drove the trail back into the woods until there was no trail. I saw a huge muddy spot and purposefully got the truck stuck there.

I killed the engine and looked at my co-conspirators and said "Let's haul ass." It was the coolest thing I ever said.

The first thing was we had to convert that topper into a boat. Dale had a thing of FlexSeal behind the seat, I'd started digging around back there looking for duct tape and saw that FlexSeal and I said "Hot damn!"

and we went around all the joints on the topper where the fiberglass meets the windows while I laid out my plan.

"I know a doctor that's got a farm not three miles south of here. This river goes right through his place. I cut hay for him sometimes. He's never there except on weekends and I figure if we can get to his place before the cops track us down we can all climb into this big RV he's got and head for Mexico and won't no one know it's missing till we're already across the border."

"This is a hare-brained scheme," said Bev.

Dale and I had the topper sealed up as good as she was gonna get. We tossed the briefcases into the upside-down topper and started carrying it to the river by an intentionally convoluted route.

"Take big squishy steps," I said. "We'll walk north a bit just to throw them off our track. Grab them rods, Bev. Grab them rods."

Dale said goodbye to his old truck. That was a sad moment.

"This is real crackpot stuff. I love you," said Bev, "but we both know you're a big dumbass and this dumbass idea is gonna land us in prison. Oh Jesus how'd I get mixed up in this?"

I didn't bother reminding her that I was the one mixed in, me and Dale, and she was the mixer. I just said "Trust me, no one floats this part of the river. You need permission from the landowners and they're all too damn stingy and hypocritical to share the river with the rest of us common folk." I shook my head. "There ain't nothing freer than a river, and these sons of bitches—"

"Stop yapping," said Dale. "Where the hell does this river even go?"

"Grand Lake, eventually. She enters there at Twin Bridges right along with the Spring River. It's a beautiful sight but we won't get to see it. We'll be cruising the open road in that doctor's RV. That should be enough footprints now, y'all get out in the water and let's head the other way."

The front end of the topper, front when it's right side up I mean, was almost square. There was a bit of an angle but you'd still call it the square end or the flat end. The back sloped out at I'd say a twenty degree angle or so. We flipped it over and made that end the bow and we had ourselves a jonboat.

"They're not gonna fall for it," said Bev. She needed a hand loading into the makeshift boat and when our hands touched there was an electric shock. We both jumped. I realized I'd leaned against some damn farmer's electric fence that had been strung real low across the river for no useful reason other than to be a dickhead.

"Not a good omen, Carl. That was not a good omen," she said.

She was fine. I climbed in and we shoved off out of the little eddy we loaded up in, out into the big beautiful muddy river. I almost had a good feeling about the whole situation.

Bev was still offering constructive criticism: "You'd have to be plumb stupid to fall for a crack-brained gambit like this."

"Have you ever met a cop, Bev?"

You could see the illumination in her eyes and in her mouth, the way it went from a scowl to a prelude to a smile.

"You know I might eat my words later, baby, but you could almost be onto something."

Just the fact of us being out on the river now, not sinking, was the most persuasive part of my argument. I think we were all a little bit skeptical but the damn thing floated. It was cozy, there was just enough room for three bank robbers, our loot, and a bird dog.

"Okay," said Bev, "now we're *really* squeezed in here."

"You know," said Dale, "fix this up with a trawling motor and rig some seats and she wouldn't be a bad little boat."

Dale always knew the right thing to say.

"Floating is nice," I said, "but I'd rather be fishing. Bev where's them rods?"

"Hush up."

She hadn't grabbed them. And we forgot the cooler. Of course there wasn't room for it anyway but I couldn't help imagining we could have somehow towed it behind us.

"A rod, a rod, my kingdom for a rod!"

I like a river that's as lazy as I am and in that particular part of southeast Kansas the Neosho River is as lazy as I am. Normally that would be great but it meant I had to paddle and all I had for a paddle was either a big stick or a small log, depending on your outlook. It was mainly only good for pushing off, I'd sink the end in the muddy bottom of the river and lever us forward and haul the stick/log/paddle in and jam it back against the river bottom and push off. It was the most convoluted method of paddling ever invented, not particularly useful in the deeper spots but still a perfect accouterment for a man who does everything in the most convoluted way possible. As sure as fish swim or nineties Chevies rust.

A fish jumped. I was sorely missing my old fishing rod. I would've done near anything for a cold beer.

"I pulled in a monster of a catfish right around this bend here," I said to no one.

"You been through here before? Why didn't you bring me?"

"You know how it is, Dale. When you ask permission to fish on someone's land you don't necessarily want to push your luck by bringing your neighbor. Especially when you didn't exactly ask permission. The good news is I know this river up and down. I could float this river in the dark. I have before."

"I'm inspired with confidence, Carl."

The thing is, she sounded sarcastic but I think she also meant it.

I am a lot of things but one thing I'm not is a liar. All the things people have said about me, that I'm a liar never has been one of them. I will tell what happened with that cop and you can believe it. I don't really feel any compunction about what happened to that policeman. In the grand scheme of existence there's no way to deny he had it coming. I have to admit I've always been somewhat prejudiced against your everyday law enforcement officer. If you ask me, a police officer is an amalgam of the two worst types of school days characters, the hall monitor and the bully. If you ask me the police in this country have too much power, they think they can get away with anything, and too many people are willing to let them. They need to be taken down a peg. Damn cops. There's two things every red-blooded American should hate: cops and bankers. A lot of people would disagree with me. You can't talk sense to people. But here it is, the Carl's honest truth: that cop had us cornered. If you listen to him tell it he claims he was going off a hunch, but the truth is he just needed a whiz at just the right moment. We came under a bridge and there he was. He looked me straight in the eyes and all I thought was well hell. Our guns were fake and my arms were tired from paddling and we were floating on an upside down truck topper carrying too much weight in human and cash cargo. We were done for and I knew it.

I was about to tell Bev she didn't even have to say it, she was right, it was a dumbass plan and I was sorry, when that policeman's expression suddenly changed. He took to hopping around going "Oh shit shit shit" and then I saw a big ugly water moccasin on the ground in front of him. He pulled out his gun and unloaded it on the poor snake but he didn't aim real careful and he shot himself in the foot, the big dumbass. That snake was shot all into bits but unfortunately for that cop one of those bits still had two fangs and a dose of venom and when he reached down to grab his wounded foot he lost his balance and fell and landed with his face next to the flopping snake head and damn if that snake didn't get its revenge. The sucker bit him right in the face. Don't tread on me and all that.

We hauled ass out of there, I mean to the extent hauling ass was possible. I shove-paddled until my fingers bled and then I just kept shove-paddling. I don't have any soft feelings for cops and especially not for that one, but I was glad to hear he didn't die and highly irritated to hear that he was claiming we had shot him, that we had initiated a shootout. No, he as good as had us but unlike Dale he had no grace under pressure. He lost his nerve because he was too much a cop.

Nothing real eventful happened after that, other than we spooked a couple herons that weren't used to humans floating through their hunting grounds. Mainly we just shot the shit while we calculated the odds on whether we could get to the doc's place before the cops could get a boat in the water.

"I didn't know it at the time but when I lived down in Joplin I lived right up the street from the Bonnie and Clyde house. There's a historical marker sign there now that wasn't there before. Bonnie and Clyde holed up in this garage apartment for twelve days. Cool little garage. Eventually someone called the cops on them and there was a shootout where they killed two cops and got away. It's a shame they don't teach you this kind of history in school, you just have to find out about it when you get out of school, and a lot of folks just don't. Shame."

"Really?" said Bev. "Someone called the cops on old Bonnie and Clyde? *Really?*"

"Yup. Interesting fact. I swear I learned more history within a month after I graduated high school than I ever did in all my years of school. Another interesting fact—"

"I just can't get over it," she said. "Imagine being the stuckup teacher's pet who called the cops on Bonnie and Clyde. Thing is, I'll be you that ninety-five percent of the sons of bitches who run around bragging about being outlaws and rebels would call the cops on old Bonnie and Clyde."

"You know, that's us," said Dale. "Bonnie and Clyde and their third wheel."

It had probably been an hour since we saw that cop and so far there was no sign of any more, but we were on alert. I think we probably went twenty full minutes without saying anything right before I brought up Bonnie and Clyde, and for this bunch that's got to be a record. We were all feeling nervous I think but also allowing a little bit of hope to creep back into our souls. Or at least I was.

"I got a question, Carl. How we even gonna know when we get to the doc's place?"

"It's easy," I said. "You can see his house from the river. No way you could miss it."

This will seem like a narrative device but I shit you not it's true: just at that moment we slid around a little bend and the doctor's house came into view. His stately manor is what he liked to call it but it was nothing more than a monstrosity. Too big. Too showy. But whatever, the doc was nice enough. Treated me good and threw me a lot of farm work and he paid okay.

I steered us toward the bank, took longer than normal but we made it. I stayed in the river after everyone was on shore with the loot. I pushed the boat out toward the middle and we watched it sail away.

"I'm almost gonna miss that boat," said Dale.

"I ain't," said Bev. "Where's that damn RV? Let's go y'all, let's go!"

We hustled up to the metal barn the doc had built to store the RV. If we'd been thinking better we would have left the loot down by the river and just driven the RV over, but we were pretty frantic at that point. We lugged them heavy briefcases and the cash we'd stole from the Irish, which was about $50,000, all the way up the hill.

We were really lucky in that the doctor had left the keys just sitting in a cup holder. I mean, I had a key to his house anyway and I could've just walked up to the house and got the RV keys off the pegboard where he stored all his many keys, but I was dog-tired and I didn't want to walk that far.

They were all watching me, Bev and Dale and even Duke, as I warmed up to start that engine. The problem, once I turned the key, was it didn't want to start. I tried it three or four times and then I lifted the tip of my old Bass Pro hat and scratched my head for a second. There was a process to get her started, but I was following it and I couldn't think of anything I was forgetting.

"What's the hold-up, sweet cheeks? We should be moving. Let's get moving."

"I don't know, this usually works."

I tried her again. It was like that RV was an old dog that you nudge to wake up and it lifts its head up ever so slightly and looks at you for one second and lays its head down and goes back to sleep.

"Oh this ain't good," said Bev. "No sir."

My daddy used to say about me "That boy could break an anvil." Bev knew how to get to me but there was nothing she ever said that cut me like that. That man could fix anything, all I ever wanted was for him to be proud of me, and all these years later if I let myself dwell on that expression of his I could just break down, that's the power he has over me still. I could hear him in that RV, whispering from the grave in a ghostly voice, "Thaaaaaaaaat booooooooooooooooy could breeeaaaaaaak an aaaaaaaaaaaaaaaannnnviiiiiilllllll." I almost lost it. That old engine just about beat me, until Dale said "Whack it good. Give it a good whack." So I did. Right on the console, one good resounding whack. I looked at them and said "I don't care what you believe, we're gonna close our eyes and all hold hands and pray to whoever that she starts. On the count of three you say 'Amen.' One. Two." On three we said "Amen" and nothing happened. Damn them two robbers looked defeated.

"Hang on," I said, and I popped the hood. "I know one more little trick."

"What is it?"

"It'd take longer to explain than to just go do it. Just trust me. You just watch and you'll see."

I'm always happy to lay out a plan when I got one but my plan was to just act like I had a plan and hope for a miracle. What some people might cynically call a fool's luck, others might refer to as providence, or serendipity, one of them types of words. It all depends on your outlook. It always depends on your outlook.

I knocked around in that engine for a minute or two, twisting this, banging on that, and it was good they couldn't see me over the hood because I had no idea what I was meant to be doing, and then I saw it. I don't know squat about engines but there was a bigass mud dauber nest in some sort of tube. I generally try not to bother mud daubers since they're the only known predator of the black widow, but I made an exception. I dug at it and knocked it with a stick until it come loose. Those mud daubers, they're not aggressive, and they have some real benefits, but they can be a nuisance. They'll make a nest in anything. A gutter. Your nice pretty new wind chimes. The seat of your kayak if you don't take it out on the water enough. Speaking of seats you might have heard about this technique called perineum sunning, it sure don't have a catchy name, where you take off all your clothes and point your butthole straight at the sun, I don't know if it's a natural Vitamin D suppository or what. I am not here to judge or offer my opinion, although I bet it feels pretty good every once in a while, but just don't do it in mud dauber country. People talk about cockroaches outlasting us but I promise you when the humans are gone the earth will turn into one gigantic mud dauber nest.

I hollered "Hey Bev, try her now, hon" just as confident-sounding as could be. Bev slid over in the driver's seat and turned the key and for one split-second, a split-second that was also an eternity, I lost all hope and believed in nothing because nothing I did ever worked out right and it was clear that infernal engine was not going to turn over—but then it did. That old RV grumbled to life. Dale took the honor of driving us out of there. He'd signed up as the getaway driver, after all. Bev was like to strangle me she was so ecstatic. To be honest, if she strangled me I wouldn't mind, if the last feeling I ever feel is her arms around my neck and her face against my head and her boobies smushing up against me I don't think I'd see anything to complain about.

"I hate to leave that truck," said Dale.

"You can buy a new one," said Bev. "A nicer one. No offense."

"It was a good truck, Dale," I said.

Dale pulled out onto the empty highway. We had a lot of miles ahead of us and no one on our trail.

There wasn't nothing to do so I thought I'd prod Dale some more on his ethics around meat consumption since all I got was a shifty answer before. "So what's the story, Dale?" I said. "How is it a good old boy like you turned out to be a vegetarian who buys hamburgers for his dog?"

"Well," he said, and he looked at me a beat. He instinctively petted the dog on its head. What he really needed was to take a drag on a cigarette at that moment, to make it more cinematic, but of course he didn't smoke. None of us smoked. I sort of pictured him doing that though, and he took long enough to pick up his sentence that he definitely could have taken a drag off a smoke, a pretty long one. "My philosophy is if I ain't hungry enough to kill an animal, I don't deserve to eat it. I've tried but I can't kill a deer, and I don't think I could kill a cow, or even a chicken really. Old Duke, on the other hand, I'm sure would be happy to, so he deserves to eat it."

"Damn it, Dale," I said. "Damn it if that don't make more sense than I expected. Damn it."

Bev asked if I was about to go vegetarian and I said no, but I didn't have a lot of faith in my answer until Dale said, "I don't mind killing a fish, though. Go figure." And then I thought that nothing really matters. Of course it probably matters to a cow. Damn it. Damn it. Damn it, Dale.

"Pescatarian," he said. "If you want to be precise pescatarian is the word for it."

"That sounds like a religion," I said. "Actually it sounds like a dirty word."

"Well it's not."

We drove. On and on. Only stopped for gas. I put it all on my credit card since I was never going to make another payment on it. We figured Dale was the least likely of us to be recognized if we'd made the news, so we sent him in to a truckstop with the Irish cash to get food and pop and an atlas, and beer, but aside from that we only stopped for gas. I guess there were a couple truck stops that had little dog runs and Dale would let Duke out real quick to do his business.

I took the second shift. The road just went on and on. My co-conspirators were all asleep. Even the dog was asleep. I got to thinking about my dad. I wasn't much of a ballplayer. I was always off-kilter, swinging off my back foot, a strikeout king, forever batting ninth. I found myself, in a little league game, up in the count three and oh with bases loaded, bottom of the ninth, two outs, tie game. The type of high-pressure, high-glory situation you fantasize about when you're kicking around the yard tossing up rocks and swinging at them with sticks. The type of situation that marks you as a hero or a loser. I swung away. Come to find out this was against the coach's signal to take, but I didn't understand his crazy signaling system so I just stood there looking goofy and nodded my head like I knew what the hell he meant by tugging on his ear three times instead of scratching his butt like normal. And when that big meatball come across the middle of the plate I swung for the fences and that was enough to knock the ball on a soft line drive barely over the short stop's glove. For once, I was a hero. After the excitement, the high fives, the shaking hands with our opponents, I found my dad in the crowd and he put a hand on my head. Some farmer come up to him, didn't say a word to me, and said "Hey Mick was that your boy knocked in the winning run?" And Daddy said "Uh-huh. It's like they say, the sun still shines on a dog's ass."

All I could think was there was still time for something to go wrong. Except it didn't. I couldn't wrap my head around it.

The border just sort of snuck up on us and blew right past us. We had pictured something more dramatic. Leading questions, a search of the RV, a suspicious border cop. Come to find out that mainly happens on your way out of Mexico, and on your way in it's all pretty laissez-faire. It was almost a letdown, but a letdown of the good kind, and it didn't take long for it to just turn into straight-up relief. I pulled the RV over in a parking lot. We didn't know where we were going but we were free and we were loaded.

Bev grabbed my face and said "Kiss me you galoot" and I did. And I did it again. And again. God that woman. I was reeled in, ready to be gutted, breaded, and fried up. I almost asked her to marry me right there but I decided that's what that cop would do. I kept my composure. I stayed cool even though I wasn't.

Dale goes, "Now that was a midlife crisis for the books. Always knowed mine would be a doozy."

Bev laughed and she leaned over and gave Dale a kiss on the cheek, then she pulled me out of the driver's chair and said "Cabo, Dale. Take us to Cabo." Dale goes "Do you have any idea—" but she didn't hear him. She took me to the bed in the back of the RV and screwed my brains out as we rolled on through Mexico. That's what I told her, I said "I don't got no brains left. You screwed em all out."

She laughed. She liked that. She nestled up against me. We were still naked, sweating under the sheets. What a feeling. I could've used a beer but I was too happy to get up and get one.

"We did it. I almost didn't think it would work but we did it," she said. "You did it."

"Well you know what they say," I said.

"What do they say baby?"

"It don't matter," I said.

"Now what kind of a thing is that to say?"

Many many many thanks to Monica Wang, Tiffany Beliu, Yousef Allouzi, Travis Cravey, DeMisty D. Bellinger, Jason Gong, Jeff Chon, Jennifer Wortman, Joey Poole, Josh Olsen, Eric Williams, Alan ten-Hoeve, Kim Palsat, Stu and Holly, Garry Somers, Cavin B. Gonzalez, Zac Smith, and Mythic Picnic. It isn't much, but this book is for Virginia, George, and Oscar, my whole world.

Alan Good is a writer and freelance proofreader. His work has been published in *Timothy McSweeney's Internet Tendency*, *Atticus Review*, and *The Dead Mule School of Southern Literature*, to name a few. He is the print editor at Malarkey Books and also runs the extremely small press Death of Print. Educated at the University of Colorado in Boulder and The City College of New York, he taught writing at the Community College of Denver for nearly ten years. He lives in the country with his wife and children. His other books are *Mere Malarkey* and *The War on Xmas*.

alangood.net
@TheAlanGood